MW00465300

POTTED MEAT

POTTED MEAT

a novel by

STEVEN DUNN

Tarpaulin Sky Press
CA ∴ CO ∴ NY ∴ VT
2016

Potted Meat
© 2016 Steven Dunn
ISBN-13: 978-1-939460-06-6
Printed and bound in the USA

Cover art by Angel Whisenant, Norfolk, VA.
www.angelwhisenant.com

Tarpaulin Sky Press
P.O. Box 189
Grafton, Vermont 05146
www.tarpaulinsky.com

For more information on Tarpaulin Sky Press trade paperback
and hand-bound editions, as well as information regarding distribution, personal orders, and catalogue requests, please visit our
website at tarpaulinsky.com.

For my sister, Keshia Dunn

who was kind enough to bury
her imaginary friend, Carlos
every day, in an ivory
tomb of dominoes.

She never knew how Carlos died.
Or why he came back to life.

INGREDIENTS: MECHANICALLY SEPARATED CHICKEN, BEEF HEARTS, PARTIALLY DEFATTED PORK FATTY TISSUE, SALT, PEOPLE HEARTS, RAT TURDS, BELTS, CHURCH, COAL, BATS, FLOWERS, DUST, EYES, LINOLEUM, NAILS, SNAKES, GROUNDHOGS, CRAYONS, MULLBERRIES, MOONSHINE, CIGARETTES, CORPSES, TAR, BLOOD, BONES, TREES

1. LIFT TAB
2. PEEL BACK
3. ENJOY CONTENTS

1. LIFT TAB

DRAW, COLOR, MEDDLING KIDS, HAPPY LITTLE TREES, HEAVY D, DUST, SHAKE TO ERASE, TWO TIMES TWO, SHADE, BUNT, DANCE, WE, YELLOW, PLAYGROUND, WHO KNOWS, TROUBLE, NIGHT

DRAW

Every day after me and Grandad sit on the porch and eat fried green tomatoes, my cousin teaches me how to draw. He makes dashed lines in the shapes of skyscrapers, men with gold chains, girls with big breasts. I connect the dashes until the picture is complete. My cousin tells me to get a new sheet of paper and draw what I just traced. I do. He says, You need to work on your buildings but you draw some good titties.

Grandma is in the living room. She usually smells like cottage cheese. But today she smells like chitlins. I eat so much vinegar with my chitlins my lips turn white. Grandma lights a long cigarette and stabs herself in the stomach with needles. She says it's insulin. She listens to a gospel song and sings, I'm coming up on the rough side of the mountain. My cousin says, She plays that goddamn song every day. She does. I like it. I ignore him and keep drawing titties.

The next day after me and Grandad sit on the porch and eat fried green tomatoes, my cousin gives me another lesson. He makes dashed lines in the shapes of a man with a knife, a woman in a bathtub, a keyhole. I don't want to trace these shapes. He grabs my hand and makes me. He tells me to get a new sheet of paper and draw what I just traced. I don't. He grabs my hand again. He says, You need to work on your stab wounds.

I run through the house crying. I want to tell Grandma but she's stabbing herself in the stomach. I run outside and tell Grandad. He stops playing cards with his friends and takes me in the garden. Here, he says, have a little wine. I need

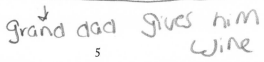
grand dad gives him wine

to tell you something. Grandad explains. When your cousin was five he saw some shit that messed him up. So don't worry too much about it, he been drawing that shit for years. Grandad tells his friends, Card game cancelled—gotta fry some tomatoes for my boy here. See you suckas tomorrow, and dont forget my goddamn money nigga.

My cousin is an artist. He says, You draw some good knives but you still need to work on your stab wounds. Lemme get one of them tomatoes. Check out my new Air Jordans. You need to learn how to rap. She plays that goddamn song every day.

COLOR

In class I sit behind Rhonda. She always raises her hand. I get to stare at her arm. I kick the back of her seat so she can turn around. I can look at the side of her face. I keep going to the pencil sharpener in the front so I can look at her eyes when I walk back. *Crush on Rhonda (?)*

I draw two pictures the same. One for me, one for Rhonda. I draw us holding hands in front of a house. Out of the chimney comes smoke shaped like hearts. A big puffy apple tree beside the house. On the tree is a heart with our initials. I start to color. Rhonda first. Hair yellow. Skin peach. I give Rhonda the picture. She smiles. *draws Rhonda a pic*

I run up the steps to my house with the picture flapping. My mom looks but don't say nothing. She shows my stepdad and says, Look at this shit. What the fuck, my stepdad says. He shoves a black crayon into my hand. His fat hand grabs mine and makes me color over Rhonda's yellow hair. Same to her face with a brown crayon. He says, Now thats better. My mom says, Shonuff is.

dont like that Rhonda's white

7

MEDDLING KIDS

The cable is off again. Me and my sister turn the knob to all thirteen channels, nothing but static. I aint playing Barbies with you, she says, cuz last time you made He-Man beat up Barbie. Good, I say, I dont wanna play that stupid shit anyway. Well, she says, I'll just pretend to watch teevee. Thats stupid, I say.

My sister sits in front of the teevee. The static is loud. She leans in and says, Zoinks. I sit next to her, What are you watching. None of your bees wax, she says. She starts singing, We got some work to do now. Can I watch too, I say. Okay, she says, but only if you be Shaggy and Scooby, and I'll be the smart ones.

She puts her hands on the steering wheel and says, Gang, we're almost to West Virginia. The mayor called us to investigate a couple of monsters thats been scaring kids all over town. I say, Ruh-roh, Raggy. My sister goes on, Lets split up and look for clues. Velma and Daphne, come with me. Shag and Scoob, start at the cemetery. I chatter my teeth and say, Ruh-roh, not the remetery. My sister says, Gang, we found some clues. We followed a little ugly boy a pretty girl into a house. We spotted the monsters when they chased the boy and girl out of the house yelling, I'll give you something to cry for. So gang, heres the plan. My sister whispers something in my ear I can't understand. Then she says, Got it Shaggy and Scoob. Zoinks, I say.

Okay gang, my sister says, we will rescue the kids from the house. But first we gotta sneak in and set up booby traps. My sister stops to think. Okay, she says, I got it now. We will go in and let the monsters see us rescuing the kids. Then they will chase us. Scoob, while theyre chasing us I want you to take this rope and trip them. I say, No way Fred. My sister goes into the kitchen and comes back with a cracker and says, How about a Scooby snack. She throws the cracker in the air and I try to catch it in my mouth but it falls on the floor. I pick it up and eat it. She goes on, After Scoob trips them with the rope, there will be oil and banana peels on the ground and they will slide down a ramp into a dumpster filled with nails and rats and barb wire. And thats when we will take they masks off.

We run through the house saying Zoinks and Yikes. We jump on the couch and dive off. We stick our heads around a corner and run in place. We run in and out of closets. My sister says, Now, Scoob. I put the jump rope in my mouth and dive in front of the door. My sister says, Whooaa—slippy-slip, down the ramp they go. She makes the deep voice of the monsters, Why is these rats bitin my ass—Who put barb wire in this goddamn dumpster. My sister grabs a baseball bat and opens the trashcan. She says, These monsters look like our mom and stepdad. C'mon Shaggy, take them goddamn masks off.

(Cable is off, prentending
to watch TV
(Scooby doo)
(barn pgs)

HAPPY LITTLE TREES

Bob Ross is on. He has paint. I don't. First I grind flowers with a rock but it don't work. I chew and chew dandelions. Spit mixes into yellow paste. I chew grass. I chew mulberries. I chew wild onions. They don't make color so I swallow. Tingles back of the neck and waters my eyes. Chew coal. Chew red clay. Chew what a grasshopper chews. I chew a grasshopper. Crunchy, then juice squirts to back of throat. The paste is chunky brown green white. Lick off hand and chew until smooth. Open jar, chew lightning bugs. Wait till night when they light, then rip off the ass, smear it on my face.

Trying to make paint out of things found outdoors

HEAVY D

I'm trying to teach my sister a song I recorded off the radio.
Listen real close, I say, One two, tell me what you got—let
me slip my coin inside your slot and hit the jackpot.

One two, she says, tell me something about coins and a
jackpot.

Goddammit, I say, you got it wrong—its not that hard.

Shut up, she says, this is stupid. Why do I need to learn this
anyway.

Cuz its important like the Pledge of Allegiance.

I know the chorus, she says, Now that we found love what
are we gonna doo.

That aint enough, I say. You gotta learn the whole thing.

Why. Since you already know it, you rap and I sing.

No. What if I cant talk one day. And if you dont know it,
then who will.

Okay, she says, just go slow next time.

I rap the first two lines. She gets it. I add more. She gets
that. After an hour she gets the last lines: I'm not quite sure
of what is going down, but I'm feeling hunky-dory bout this
thing that I found. I rewind the tape and we rap the song
three times perfect.

11

She says, If you actually found love what would you do with it.

Thats a stupid question.

No it aint, she says. Just answer it. What would you do with love.

DUST

My mom and stepdad have a baby so we move in with my stepdad's mama. The house is built on the side of a hill. The house is leaning. The house has a kitchen floor that is slanted with the tops of nails pushing through brown linoleum. The house has a basement with a coal furnace. The house is white with two bedrooms upstairs, a bedroom and kitchen and living room downstairs. My mom and stepdad and the baby sleep in the living room. LaShawn and Jamar are my stepdad's niece and nephew. They sleep in the bed with my stepdad's mama in the bedroom on the first floor. In the same room me and my sister sleep on the floor. Nobody sleeps upstairs.

When I put coal on the fire before bed a rat waddles along the wooden beams and stops to look down at me. Now while I'm trying to sleep I hear the rat scratching and chewing wood under the floor.

At five my stepdad yells to wake me to put coal on the fire. He says I didn't fix it good enough last night at one. He says if I fixed it good enough I could sleep till five-thirty. I walk outside and go to the basement. I shovel two buckets of ashes from the bottom of the furnace and dump them over the hill. Then I fill seven buckets of coal and dump three on the fire so it will last until I come from school.

Me and my sister, and LaShawn and Jamar, come from school. My stepdad yells because the fire went out. He said he and his mama and the baby was cold all day. That I was trying to freeze them to death. LaShawn and Jamar ask me why can't I fix the fire right. My mom tells me I better get my

13

shit together. I go to the basement and the fire is out. I put too much coal on and smothered it. I need to build a new fire.

There's an old house next door where I get dry wood. With the axe I chop brittle walls, Kick through walls, chop up the floor. Awake the rats. Their nest is tangled straw, sticks, and dry leaves. In it is chewed up Bible pages. Empty can of potted meat. Cracked pork chop bones. Half-eaten Barbie head.

At five the next morning I put three buckets of coal on the fire so it will last until I come from school.

SHAKE TO ERASE

I did something bad, at school or at home, maybe school, probably home.

I'm thinking of how to draw a face on my Etch-A-Sketch how to draw the eyes and eyebrows without drawing a line across the top of the nose I'd have to draw one eye and make the eyebrow really bushy then from the corner of the eye I'd have to draw the nose down and around and back up and do another eye then I'd have to trace the nose back down to the bottom and make a mustache so the line won't show where it need to connect to make lips but how do I get to the chin and the outside of the face without showing a line. Start over Shake.

Stepdad hits me again, extension cord, or switch. Oh, you aint cryin. You think you a man, I'll beat you like one.

Start with the hairline then draw a beard like how I'd do the mustache then draw the lips up to the nose and eyes then do the eyebrows last trace the nose back down to the lips and chin and draw a neck then draw a city in the background draw lines up and across and down and make different sizes of skyscrapers then trace over the top of the man's head and draw more buildings on the other side then turn the knob all the way to the edge and go all the way up up and draw an airplane in the corner then turn the knob all the way over over to the other corner and draw a sun. Start over Shake.

I pull up my white long johns. Stripes soak through. Red zebra.

15

TWO TIMES TWO

My uncle, mom's brother, picks me and my friend Mack up from school early. Mack's dad is driving. He says we gotta go to Pocahontas Virginia to handle some business. He stops at the filling station. My uncle gives me and Mack some money and tells us to buy a big bag of Funyuns and Moonpies and Salem One Hundreds and a bottle of Wild Irish Rose, the big bottle.

road trip snacks

Mack's dad speeds down hill around curves while we slide back and forth across the backseat and raise our hands like on a rollercoaster and we say, Whoo, faster faster. He goes faster. We pass around the Funyuns and eat our Moonpies. Mack says, Dangit, Dad, we aint buy no sodas, I'm thirsty. My uncle hands the bottle of Wild Irish Rose to us and says, Dont drink too much, this aint no Kool-Aid.

girl share wild irish rose

With both hands Mack tips the bottle to his lips and says, Ahh, it taste like Kool-Aid. He gives me the bottle. It do taste like Kool-Aid, I say. They laugh. I give the bottle to my uncle, he drinks, gives it to Mack's dad, he drinks, gives it to Mack, he drinks, gives it back to me. It goes like this until we get to Pocahontas.

wait in car

We cross train tracks and park behind a brick building. The roof is caved in and windows half busted out. Poison ivy crawls up the side. My uncle says, You turkeys hold tight, we'll be back in a few ticks. Mack, I say, look at your dad. We make fun of Mack's dad because he has a jerry curl tied in a baby ponytail and wears the same thing every day: A red and black tracksuit and black Chuck Taylor's. His pants are high and you can see his white socks. His stomach sticks out

16

explain how uncle & macks dad look

and he never wears a shirt under his jacket. He wears a gold rope chain with a bunny on it resting in his curly chest hair. Mack says, So, look at your uncle. My uncle got on blue jean bell-bottoms with a brown leather jacket. A Blue jean floppy hat. He don't have a shirt on under his jacket either. They walk to a house with white paint peeling off. Half of the porch droops. A big Doberman is tied to a tree in the dirt yard. It keeps barking and running until the chain yanks it back.

They break window out & play baseball b/ coal

Mack says, Lets see if we can bust out the rest of the windows. We throw rocks at the top windows. Mack is the first one to hit glass. He says, Thats why I'm the pitcher and you play leftfield. So, I say, I betcha I'll hit way more than you. We throw more. He keeps hitting glass. I don't. Mack says, I wanna practice my fastball. I find a broken broomstick next to the brick building. Mack collects a shirt-full of coal and rocks from the train tracks.

Mack throws a piece of coal. I swing, but it feels real slow. I'm getting a little woobly. See, Mack says, I told you my fastball was fast. Mack raises his leg to pitch but he woobles a bit. He laughs, I dont know whats wrong with me. He throws a piece of coal high in the air. I swing. Hit. It explodes. Dust powders my face. Mack laughs. Me too. Mack throws another. I miss. Mack says, You like Rhonda donctha. Hell no, I say, who told you that. I seen that picture with yall holding hands, he says. I aint draw no picture of nobody, I say.

Whats taking them so long, I say. I dont know, Mack says, but I'm getting thirsty again. I think they left that bottle in the car, I say. We get the bottle and sit on the steps of the brick building. I drink, give it to Mack, he drinks, gives it back. It goes like this until it starts to get dark. You ever smoke before, Mack says. I took a puff of my uncles Salem one time, I say. I smoke all the time, he says. We search the car for the Salems but don't find none. We can smoke leaves, Mack says, my cousin do it all the time. Mack tears a piece of paper out of his notebook. He picks some poison ivy off of the building. He rolls it into the paper and licks the seam. Thats nasty, I say, I dont wanna smoke your spit. I have to do that, he says, so it will stick. Mack lights the paper. He sucks on it. Coughs a little cough. Smoke rolls out his nose and mouth. He gives it me. I do the same but don't cough. Mack says, You didnt inhale. You gotta make the smoke go in your lungs. I try again. Take a deep breath, Mack says. I choke. Smoke shoots out my mouth and nose. I drool on my shirt. Eyes water. I look at Mack. His face is melting. Mack smokes, gives it to me, I smoke, give it back. It goes like this until Mack's dad and my uncle stumble out with their arms around each other. Their slow brown faces laughing and smoking.

In the car Mack's dad says, What happened to all the Rose. My uncle laughs and says, Them turkeys drunk it all. Oh well, Mack's dad says. My uncle says, Shit, we forgot to tell yall turkeys do ya homework. What yall got anyway. Um, I say, we sposed to be learning our times tables. Oh yeah, Mack says, we gotta do these worksheets. I hate times tables, I say, its too hard. My uncle says, Aw hell, it aint that damn hard. He takes out a pack of Salems and says, Look, its twenty cigarettes in this one pack. If you had two packs how many would that be. Forty, I say. Good, he says, you just did twenty times two. Now if you had three packs, how many is that. Mack says, Sixty. Good, my uncle says, thats twenty times three. Now do the same with all the times tables, just keep adding. See, that shit is easy aint it. Mack's

18

dad turns the yellow light on in the top of the car so we can do the worksheets. All the way home my uncle makes us recite all the twos to the twelves over and over.

Mack's dad drives up on the hill to drop me and uncle off. Everybody is in the street with the sheriff. My mom runs up and slaps my uncle in the face, Where the hell yall been, she says, I thought his dad kidnapped him, why you aint tell nobody you picked him up, you drunk muthafucka. My uncle says, Be cool, jack. That boy is fine. My mom slaps him again. My uncle says, I said chill the fuck out. He did his homework and we fed him. My mom says, I had enough of you, you fuckin drunkard, got my kid runnin the streets, had me thinkin his dad kidnapped him. My uncle grabs my shoulders and kisses me on the forehead. He hugs me and says, Alright turkey, get some rest and have a good day at school tomorrow. My lungs and my throat feel weird. My mom grabs me and says, Look at me boy, whats wrong with you. I throw up on her feet.

SHADE

Chrissy Ann hears someone say she stinks. She goes to the corner of the playground and kicks the fence. I ask her whats wrong. Nothing, she says. I ask her if she is coming to baseball practice. I already know she is because her dad and my stepdad are the coaches. They say her dad is racist but he is always nice to all the black people on our team. She asks can she wear my hat. I give it to her. Blondish brown hair hangs out. Whats this X stand for, she says. Malcolm X, I say. Who is that.

Buck runs over and says, Stinking bitch, you smell like wolf pussy. How do you know what wolf pussy smells like, she says, wolves aint even in West Virginia. Yeah, I say, wolves only live in the North Pole, you stupid muthafucka. So, Buck says, you still stink.

Chrissy Ann don't stink. She smells like work. Like how I smell like coal smoke. She lives at the end of the holla on top of a mountain and has lots of hogs and chickens. She feeds them every morning. When I was at her house her little brother stuck a stick up the hog's butt. Chrissy Ann slapped the shit out of him. Then she hugged the hog. Then she said we should take a walk in the woods to get out the heat and away from her stupid brother.

We stroll through old trees. Dirt is black and soft. Dark green ferns and bright green moss. We pick blackberries and blow on them before eating. Mushrooms the size of saucers. Not for eating, she says, but to keep cool. She rubs the mushroom on her forehead and cheeks. Tells me to. The brown inside of the mushroom feels like a damp sponge.

She picks another and rubs it on her neck and arms. Grabs my wrist and rubs the mushroom on the inside of my arm. My neck. She presses her lips against mine and pushes her tongue in my mouth. It tastes like blackberries. Is this okay, she says. Yeah, I say. We look at my shorts poking out. She smells like mushrooms and hogs.

BUNT

My stepdad has a long white Chrysler with cushy green seats. He picks all the kids up on our baseball team from all their houses. We pile onto each other's laps. Music is blasting and laughing while he swings the car around curves. He starts practice by hitting balls to us in the infield, then outfield. The ting of the ball on the aluminum bat sounds like the slap on my forearm for mosquitoes. Then we run laps, giving him a high-five each time we round home plate. On the way home he buys each of us a bag of chips. He does the same thing the next day and the next day. He does the same thing during football season.

Talks about what they do at baseball practice

DANCE

Jamar and my sister are in the same class. We come from school and Jamar tells everybody that my sister stood on her desk and took her clothes off and sang, Do the Humpty-Hump. She was just like this, he says and stands in the chair and twists his hips and rubs his stomach while pulling up his shirt. My mom says to my sister, You a whore, huh, showin ya ass in public. Jamar keeps dancing on the chair and saying, Yep, she was just like this.

Some words are boiling in my belly and pushing up through my chest, my chest tries to trap these words, but these words keep pushing up like puke, and my mouth spews, Stop fuckin lying Jamar.

Watch ya fuckin mouth, my mom says, who told you talk when aint nobody talkin to ya little dumb ass. Stupid mutha-fucka, my stepdad says, you the fuckin liar. You gonna get it now, my mom says. LaShawn and Jamar laugh. My stepdad says, I know thats right, you betta whoop his ass before he try to whoop yours.

My mom tells me to pull my pants down and bend over the stool. She is having a hard time choosing between the belt and the extension cord. Until my stepdad says, Use this, and gives her a big stick. I'm thinking of how to draw a face on my Etch-A-Sketch.

23

WE

Last night I dreamed that me and my sister were in front of the house playing hopscotch. After I won, cuz I always win, we sat on the porch. We were laughing. Somebody drives up and shoots my sister in the chest.

I wake up the next day and while we walk down the hill to the bus stop I keep looking at my sister to see if she is okay. She looks at me and says, You okay. Yeah, I say, why. Cuz, she says, Last night I had a dream that me and you was in front of our house playing hopscotch. And after I won, cuz I always win, we was sitting on the porch laughing. And somebody drove up and shot you in the chest.

[handwritten margin note: Sister had same exac dream]

YELLOW

Everyone is downstairs crying. I walk upstairs to Grandma's room. It is dark. Her dirty pink house shoes are lined up by the nightstand like she just got into bed. The covers on her side are pulled back like she just got out of bed. I leave and ask my mom how Grandma died. My mom says she just turned yellow and died. What, I say. You heard me, she says, she just turned yellow and died. I will never eat dandelions again.

PLAYGROUND

We have a new girl that just moved from Africa. Gambia. I looked it up in my atlas and it looks like a crooked little finger in the middle of Senegal. Her name is Anter Jatta. I say it over and over. Anter Jatta. She is really dark and pretty. Everybody else says she is black and ugly. Buck says she is so black if she wore yellow lipstick she would look like a cheeseburger. He says this in front of her because she don't understand English that much. She smiles. Her teeth are really white and straight.

I make sure I wear my African sign everyday. I even wear my afro pick with the fist on the end. At recess by the monkey bars I say to her, My beautiful Sister, what is it like in the Mother Land. The man tries to hold us down in America. I know about Senegal too. She smiles.

I walk back to the basketball court and Buck says, I see you over there tryin to hook up with that African booty scratcher. No way, I say, I was just telling her how black she was. Its okay to hook up with her, he says. Buck knows a lot because this is his third time in sixth grade. He explains, She probably got some wet jungle pussy, its neon pink. Can you imagine how wet that pussy hair is. You can swing from it like vines. All African girls cut they pussy hair in the shape of a African sign, they even dye it red, yellow, and green.

When recess is over, me and Buck walk by Anter Jatta. I raise my fist and say, Solid. Buck says, Whats up, jungle pussy. She smiles.

26

WHO KNOWS

We have one homeless man in our town. Everybody calls him the Man in Black. Because that's all he wears is black, most of the black is coal dust, plus he is dark skinned. He is really tall and his dirty hands look like bear paws and his big boots thud the ground with each stride. He lives in a saggy brown canvas tent next to the creek at the bottom of the mountain. In the winter you can see the blue flame from his kerosene heater glowing inside the tent. He never talks to nobody.

I see him in the store sometimes buying bread and baloney with a hundred dollar bill. Thats because he gets a crazy check, they say. Some people say he went crazy in the war. Some say he just went crazy. Some say he sold his soul to Satan. My uncle says he is a righteous revolutionary brother who spits in the man's face. My grandma says he used to be married to a white woman and she took everything he had and now he don't want shit to do with nothing white, especially no stankin-ass white folks.

When I'm behind the Man in Black in the store he stinks so bad my stomach hurts. He turns around, looks down at me, sees me frowning and covering my nose, and says, I dont smell no worse than ya drunk ass uncle.

TROUBLE

My aunt, mom's sister, says me and my sister are in trouble and we need to come down to her house asap. I already know why. And I told my dumb ass sister not to call the Care Bear Hotline. Imma whoop yalls ass good when you get back, my mom says, You ran up her phone bill a hundred dollars. My aunt says, Dont worry, Imma take care of it.

While we walk to our aunt's house I keep telling my sister she is stupid and I'm gonna say I aint have shit to do with it. She knows our stepdad don't like us going down there, and you done fucked it up, I say. Shut up, she says, You was there so its your fault too.

We walk in our aunt's house and she is sitting on the couch with the phone bill on top of a book in her lap. She takes off her glasses, Why'd you do it. My sister says, I dont know, I'm sorry. I know youre sorry, she says, but you know why you called the Care Bears. Um, my sister says, I guess I just wanted to talk. Well, my aunt says, dont worry, this is a diminutive problem we can take care of. Diminutive is my aunt's favorite word. She says it a lot. Especially when she talks about her shot glasses she collects when she travels. Cmon in the kitchen, she says. We walk through the hall past her long bookshelf. Oh, she says, I have a glass from San Francisco to add to my diminutive glass collection.

My aunt starts frying fish and telling me and my sister about a new book she is reading. A moving mystery, she says, but with literary sensibilities. I'm trying to write a book too, I say, it's kind of a mystery, cuz I don't know what's going to happen, its diminutive so far cuz I just started, but I want it to be not diminutive when I finish. Well hell, she says, you gotta show me this book.

We all sit at the kitchen table eating fried fish, hot sauce and little bones and grease everywhere. My aunt leaves and comes back with the telephone. Here, she says to my sister, you can call them again if you want.

Aunt is
okay w/ them
calling Care bear
hotline

NIGHT

Everyone is talking about a ninja that's creeping around at night and hunting kids. Dont go out after the streetlights come on, they say, lock your doors and keep your guns loaded.

That's stupid. Ninjas don't hunt kids. And if a ninja is looking for kids that means he is trying to find a worthy student. Maybe he seen me doing my moves in the yard. My roundhouse is good. Dropkick is perfect. Backflip needs work.

I will keep practicing so he can take me back to Japan. I checked my globe. And from West Virginia, if going east to Japan, it takes twenty-three fingersteps. If going west it takes sixteen and a half. On the globe Japan is 135 degrees east longitude and 37 degrees north latitude. Almost the same latitude as West Virginia. So maybe Japan has the same deciduous forest and the ninja wants a student that can navigate this type of terrain. He will take me on a hike to a village way up in the foggy mountains and I will train for a whole year. I will miss seventh grade. So the fuck what. I will get to throw ninja stars into people's throats. Shoot arrows in squirrel eyes. Hang upside down from trees. Tippy toe around at night. Kill people.

I saw him one evening sneaking up the side of mountain. That's where he watches me from so I switch my training to the back yard. With coal buckets filled with rocks I do twenty curls with each arm. Then I put a broomstick through the handles and do fifty squats. Twenty kicks with each leg on the clothesline pole. I make nun chucks by cutting my dog's chain with bolt cutters and taping it to two sticks with electrical tape. I do the same workout for two weeks but the

30

ninja never comes. He wants me to find him. The final test
is to prove my tracking skills.

I wait till everyone is asleep and sneak out with my nun
chucks tucked into the back of my black sweatpants, black
hoodie, black skull cap. My shoes are white, but dirty. I keep
looking behind me to make sure no one is watching. My
dog tries to follow. I put my finger to my lip and say, See you
next year. Step over the train tracks, take off my shoes, roll
up my pants, wade across the creek. Moonlight helps me see.
I smell smoke and see the glow of a fire at the top. I snap a
twig. Dart behind a tree. Shit, too much noise. Breath slower
so he won't hear my heart beat. Look up in the tree to make
sure he aint tracking me. I step from behind the tree. Snap
another twig. Roll over to another tree. Lay on my stomach.
With my nun chucks I sweep the twigs out the way and use
my forearms to inch myself up the hill. Sniff soil to see if I
can pick up his scent. Nothing but little balls of deer shit.
Keep pulling myself up, sweep away twigs, crawl. Dirt piles
up inside the top of my pants. I finally reach the top at a
small clearing. My back against a tree. Peek around and see
him leaned up against a rock with his back to me. The fire
is dying. He knows I'm coming. Ninja, I whisper, its me,
your faithful disciple. He doesn't turn around. Ninja. Master
Ninja. I have come to learn the ways of the night. He doesn't
move. Move closer. His mask is on the rock. He has an afro.
I peek over his shoulder and recognize his face. It's crazy
Percy from down the road. A needle stuck in his forearm.

2. PEEL BACK

GEOGRAPHY, LOVE, TUNNEL LOVE, BIRTHDAY, MONEY,
TRAINS, IT, TEXTURE, SUPER POWERS, CONFIRMATION,
LIGHT, WHITE, GOOD OLE DAYS, BROTH, USUAL ROUTE,
JIVE ASS CHUMPS, TELL YOU A STORY, PEOPLE'S IN-
STINCTIVE TRAVELS AND THE PATHS OF RHYTHM

GEOGRAPHY

My 2nd period teacher erases the chalkboard, her butt slides side to side, calves flex as she tippy-toes, she turns, the V in her chest slopes heavy in her silk red shirt, she clicks to her chair, sits, crosses her legs, I get hard. Shift in my seat so it will rub against my pants. Page thirty-eight, she says.

My hand raises itself. I cant find Constantinople on this map, I say, can you come show me. You cannot find Constantinople because it is not on there, she says, but I'll show you where Istanbul is. She clicks over, perfume reaches me first, she bends and her heavy V spreads in front of my desk. Her liquid red fingernail circles along the page until it stops. Here is Istanbul, she says, it is the modern day city of Constantinople. Oh, I say, thanks. She walks away but her perfume lives in my mouth. She reaches up and pulls down the map. Since I just showed you, she says, please come up and show the class where Istanbul is.

Crush on teacher[?]

I tuck it into the elastic of my underwear and stand. Istanbul is the modern day city of Constantinople, Istanbul is the day of Constantinople, Istanbul is modern. I point to the map. She stands next to me. I ask can I go to the bathroom.

LOVE

Behind the house over the hill and up the side of the other hill is a groundhog family. All day I watch them waddle out the hole and eat weeds. Mister Ray likes to eat them but he's too old to hunt. He pays fifteen dollars for a fat groundhog, twenty for skinned and gutted. I need money to buy my girlfriend a necklace for her birthday.

Spray turpentine on my shoes to keep snakes away. Carry a twenty-two rifle. A sickle to chop tall stalks. Swing chop. Swing chop. Snake hangs from the mulberry tree. Raise my turpentine foot to scare it away. Doesn't work. Rub dirt on hands and grip sickle handle. Step back and measure the swing like baseball. Draw back, step, swing. Snake head drops while body squirms and squirts blood. Wipe it off my face with the back of my hand.

Sit on mound behind groundhog hole so I can blow its fucking head off. It never comes. Take same route back to avoid cutting weeds. Snake body still hangs. Stand on other hill at distance. It waddles out, sniffs air, waddles on. Chews weeds, sniffs air, chews on. Breathe in, hold, squeeze trigger. Ground hog tumbles downhill. I run to get it. Clean shot in the neck. I think the bullet went through. Plunge my finger in the hole. Mushy warm.

Flip groundhog on its back. Its full belly jiggles to a spread like a rubber hot water bottle. I saw somebody do this before. I think I can do it. Stick knife in bullet hole. Twist to make hole bigger. Saw skin and meat and cords around and around until head hangs. Hack at neck bone. Toss head in the weeds. Slip knife point in ass. Slowly slice upward to belly. Knife

36

slips too deep. Stomach spills open. Guts plop out. Keep working knife upwards to where head was. Skin unzips like a coat. Red soaked soft. Pull out all organs. Toss in the weeds. Wipe blood hands on my shorts. Get back to the house and spray groundhog with water and put in plastic bag.

I yell through the screen door, Mister Ray, I bought you a groundhog. I aint ask for no damn groundhog, he says. He tells me to come in and show him anyway. I aint know how to skin it, I say. And you aint cut the feet off either, he says, what the hell I sposed to do with a furry groundhog with feet. I tell him why I need the money. He laughs and says, Alright now, the young man tryin to get him some trim. Put that ground-hog in the Frigidaire, I'll get somebody up here to skin it. He gives me fifteen dollars. I thank him and start to walk out. Hold on now, he says. He gives me ten more, Make sure you get that gal something nice, a real nice necklace.

My cousin drives me an hour to the mall. I buy A Tribe Called Quest tape. Snoop Dogg tape. Newports. Cherry slushy.

TUNNEL LOVE

We have a brown creek that esses through, next to the train tracks at the bottom of the mountain where the tunnel curves out. Sometimes you can catch a fish. I take my uncle's pole and go down to the bank, my toes sunk in mud. The best spot is right here in the middle of the curve. On top of the washing machine. I pull my shirt off and slosh out, careful not to slip on furry rocks. Use the tire to bounce up on the washing machine. The fish live under that rock. The rock wrapped in ripped panty hose, sweat pants, blue tarp. I sit with my line, and when the fish are about to bite, they get scared by beer cans floating down and pinging the washing machine. Ping scatter Ping scatter. The tunnel spits out a train. Today it is slow, and long. Grey cars carry coal piled high into rounded pyramids. Words spray-painted on the sides. Words I can't read but look like flying dragons made of purple arrows yellow bubbles and red loops twisting all kinds of ways. Car by car by car comes out. Finally one I can read. Plain black letters say: Fuck You Tameka From Yonkers You Broke My Heart.

Sitting near the tunnel fishing, sees cars driving by

BIRTHDAY

It is that time of year again when my mom walks me and my sister to the graveyard. The graveyard is on top of the hill in the woods. We spray turpentine on our shoes and take sticks to knock weeds out the way in case of snakes.

We start up the hill, a steep drop on our left, mom in front, sister in the middle, me in back. We swing at the tops of the weeds and stomp on the bottoms so they won't pop back up. Slowly we knock down more weeds, and step, knock down more, and step, until we reach the top. Careful not to step on people's graves. Weeds and tree roots and vines cover the headstones. You can read the names if you rip off the vines.

We finally get there. It looks different this year because bright green poison ivy crawls on the rusty spiked fence around the grave. After tearing weeds off the gate we walk inside. My mom gets on her knees and pulls the roots and moss and poison ivy from the crumbled headstone. She says to my sister, like she says every year, Heres your twin, died three months after yall was born. I look at my sister. Her twin walks up and stands next to her. They are holding hands. My mom says, Why God why. I ask my mom again how she died. She just died, she says.

MONEY

I get my first summer job. On the trash truck Mondays through Friday. Four-twenty five an hour. I get up at five-thirty and meet the truck at the city hall at six. Just throw the goddamn bags in the truck, Russell says, then hit the side to let me know when you done and I'll pull off. I throw a bag in, hit the side of the truck, he pulls off. He drives slowly up hills, down hills, around curves, up hills again. Throw bag, hit truck, pull off.

Some of the bags bust. Meat and milk drip onto my chest. Diapers, chicken bones, maxi pads. I lift a bag above my head and brown jelly oozes into my mouth. Lunch time, Russell says, we behind schedule cuz of you. We'll just sit right here on the back of the truck and eat real quick. I sit with my bologna sandwich and Fritos. Gray milk, I think, soaks through my pants until I feel it in my crack and on my balls.

Russell pulls a blue cooler from behind the seat. In it are two ice cold bottles of MD 20/20. Orange Jubilee and Banana Red. He gives me the Banana Red and says, A little afternoon refreshment, good sir. Why thank you, Sir Russell, I say, you are most kind. You are most welcome, but don't think you gonna get some free shit every day, nigga.

TRAINS

My friend Reggie ran away from home, for real ran away. Everybody says it's because his dad would chain him up in the basement and whoop his ass. Some people said Reggie needed his ass beat cuz he was a fuck up. Some people said yes, he did need his ass beat, but not that bad.

Reggie's dad always comes around to the house to get drunk with my stepdad. He acts like Reggie is still chained up in the basement, like nothing ever happened. He tries to joke and is always laughing in my face with his missing teeth but he is not funny. He will never be funny.

The other day at school Buck was saying that Reggie was staying at that boys' home up the road. He said his aunt told him. And last night I heard my mom tell the same lie.

I know where Reggie is because we made the plan together. I was supposed to go too, but I got scared. Reggie said he was going to do just like on teevee, pack his shit in a red bandana and tie it to a pole. But he had his book bag when I last saw him. Then he said he was going to hop a train with the other hobos and go to Kansas City. He said he knew trains went to Kansans City because all the old songs talked about it. I stole money out of my mom's pocket book and gave it to him before he left.

IT

I can't help it. I have to play with myself every chance I get. That's how I got caught when my mom came into the bathroom. I don't know if I was making too much noise or just taking too long, but for some reason she bust in there. Then she told everybody in the house. They all laughed. Said it's a sin. They keep asking what is wrong with me. I don't know what's wrong with me. So every time I take a shit and it takes a while they think I'm playing with myself. Most of the time I am. Now I don't even wanna take a shit in the bathroom. I do it in the bushes. In buckets of ashes. On the bottom floor of the old house next door.

Miss Janet wore a short dress to Sunday school. I need to go the bathroom and play with myself. It is kinda hard to do because that big velvet picture of Jesus is looking at me. He is crying. So when I finish I go outside by the creek to take a shit. Since I'm squatting I say, Dear Jesus and God, please help me to quit playing with myself.

I go back in to the sanctuary and our pastor is yelling about how God sees everything you do. That was the lesson last week too. Miss Janet walks on stage and starts singing. I can see the dark crack between her thighs. I go back to the bathroom. It feels good. Real good. And I think that if God is watching me do this he must be a nasty motherfucker.

TEXTURE

Something tells me to stick the tip of the screwdriver into the fire. Something tells me to hold it there until it glows red. Something tells me to place the glow on the soft inside of my forearm. Something tells me to hold it there. Smells like fried chicken. My entire body lights up yellow. Something tells me to stick the screwdriver back into the fire and keep doing this until I carve an M. I don't know what M means.

My mom sees the M while I'm taking a bath. What the fuck, she says. She leaves and comes back with the extension cord.

The red welts on my dick are smooth. The M is pus-filled and lumpy.

[handwritten marginalia: Burns an M onto himself]

SUPER POWERS

Once a week, mostly twice, he gets into a fight with his mom and stepdad. They yell. He yells back, louder, louder, chest out like a gorilla, showing his large yellow teeth strung together with silver slobber. He shatters a cinderblock over his stepdad's head. His mom runs off, he lets her get to the bottom of the hill, then he squats and the ground shakes, and he leaps all the way down the hill onto her back and chokes her with the inside of his elbow while whispering in her ear that everything is okay. He flies back up to the house where his stepdad's fat body is puddled in the street with no head. The head is in front of the door yelling, yelling, yelling. He kicks it. It flies into the kennel and his dog bites one of its cheeks and shakes, shakes, shakes. His sister pokes her head out the door. He tells her he is leaving, he has to go. Everything crumbles away and a path appears. When he starts to walk he awakes, and drinks moonshine before brushing his teeth. Toothpaste makes moonshine taste like piss.

CONFIRMATION

Last week I asked my pastor if could I do a special presentation this week at Sunday School. I wanna recite the entire Psalms 23 and 24, I said, and all eight of the beatitudes. Yes, he said, its a blessing when the youth step up.

All week when I'm in the basement at night I drink moonshine while studying for my presentation. I'm taking a break from my Iceberg Slim novel, Pimp. It's getting a little scary with him beating up all those women and taking their money, or his money, I don't know whose it really is.

My pastor announces, One of our youth has a special presentation today. I stand in front of the pulpit and start with Psalms 23 and finish with 24. No mistakes, no stumbling. Loud and clear. Now I would like to continue with the beatitudes from Matthew, I say. Amen, everyone says, go head boy. I start, Blessed are the poor in spirit, for theirs is the kingdom of Heaven. Amen, they say, aint that the truth. I keep rambling them off until I get to the end. I look at the congregation, and as I expected, they look confused, perfect. I know I skipped the sixth one, I say, but I wanted to save it for last because its the most important to me. Blessed are the pure in heart, for they will see God.

Amen, everyone says. They clap. My pastor pats me on the shoulders. People hug me, We just know youre gonna be a preacher one day. I stick out my chest and grin. Youre definitely gonna be a preacher, they say, you love the lord and you can memorize the word so good.

I get home and take a sip of shine, still smiling. Yep, I can be a preacher. I know I can memorize stuff really good. I like memorizing stuff that's hard to memorize. Like Bone Thugs-n-Harmony, they rap really fast and I know all the words to First Of Tha Month . . . Hey my nigga we havin a wonderful daaay, and I won't fuck with me. Whyyy? Cause it's the 1st of the month, and now we smokin, chokin, rollin blunts and sippin on 40 ounces . . . That's a hard song to memorize.

LIGHT

A bat sneaks into the living room again. It squeaks behind the couch while we watch teevee. My stepdad says, Yall know the drill, get ya weapons and I'll hit the lights. I get my old tennis racket from the corner, Jamar grabs his baseball bat, LaShawn reaches for her badminton racket, my sister gets the broom, my mom flips open a plastic grocery bag. Grandma scoots as fast as she can to her room, her slippers and the tennis balls on the legs of her walker skid on the linoleum in the kitchen.

We station ourselves around the living room, gripping our weapons. Stepdad flips on the light and says, Go. The bat swoops up from behind the couch screeching, and flutters around the ceiling. I jump and swing, nip its wing. It dives toward the floor and Jamar takes a golf swing, misses. My sister puts the broom above her head with both hands and chops, knocking over a lamp. LaShawn half swings while she screams because the bat is flying at her face. She ducks and the bat zooms into my strike zone. I pull my racket back, release, smack the bat in the face. It shoots into the wall and drops to the carpet. My mom jumps and covers it with the plastic bag. She holds up the bag and the bat barely flaps its wings inside. Its screeches soften.

Grandma says bats have evil souls and they carry diseases. After me and Jamar spray Raid through the house we join everybody in the middle of the street to burn the bat. To get rid of the evil. We all sit in a circle. Grandma prays. The bat is half flopping in the middle. My stepdad pours kerosene on it and drops a match, poof. The bat screeches, its tiny mouth opens wide while flames shoot through its pointy teeth. Our faces glow.

WHITE

After putting coal on the fire for the night I bury my jar of moonshine in the snow. Then I pull it from its ice hole and gulp one more gulp before going in.

Mom, Stepdad, Grandma, LaShawn, and Jamar sit at the kitchen table watching a movie. I sit on the floor next to my sister. Her eyelids droop and her chin slides into her chest. I elbow her, Wake up, they're gonna see you. She opens her eyes, sits up straight. I yawn. She yawns. Again her head falls forward. Wake up, I whisper. My mom looks over, Wake up, goddammit. Stepdad says, Sleepin again, huh. Grandma says, Take your ass outside, betcha that cold air will wake you up. And dont put no coat on either. LaShawn and Jamar laugh. My sister walks out, head down.

I feel my eyes close and head fall. Reach under my shirt and pinch my stomach until fingernails fill with flesh. In the movie a boy is running from a man in a maze of bushes. The boy makes footprints in the snow by walking backwards. My head droops. Stepdad says, Muthafucka, wake up. Mom says, Take your ass outside too, and dont yall come back till you can stay awake.

My sister is on her knees in the snow. A jump rope around her throat. She is shivering. I am shivering. The slivers of space between shivers are warm. I want to gather them in my hands like sewing pins and give them to her.

From behind the house I dig out my moonshine. Take a drink, I say. It burns, she says. Good, I say. Lets make a snowman, she says.

48

GOOD OLE DAYS

It is Christmas and my aunts, stepdad's sisters, came in from New York like they do every year. The tree we decorated flashes white and red in the corner. They sit at the kitchen table drinking Bacardi, smoking cigarettes. Stepdad is drinking Wild Turkey 101. Mom is drinking beer. Me and my sister sit on the floor. We were drinking moonshine outside a few minutes ago. She got mad at me because I said, Fuck Christmas. She said, I like it because its a special time for families to act like they like each other. I said she was stupid like everybody else. She said I was stupid like everybody else too.

My stepdad and his brothers and sisters talk about all the times they got beat when they were kids. My aunt says, Remember when dad put my head between his legs and beat me with that cast iron skillet. Yeah, they all laugh, he tore your ass up. Remember, my stepdad says, when mom slapped me upside the head with that broomstick cuz I talked back. HaHaHaHa, heads back, mouths wide open. Remember, my stepdad's brother says, when I told dad I aint wanna cut grass and he ran outside with that hammer and hit me in the back. HaHaHaHa. Yeah buddy, my stepdad says, them was the good ole days. He is smiling out of one side of his mouth and is staring at the floor.

BROTH

reading Obituary & cooking

Boy get that paper and read me all the dead folks, this old woman's eyes gettin bad and this ol'arthur got my fingers all bent up. While you over here, help me get these neckbones to boiling. Who? Speak up boy.   Ernestine? MmHmm, that aint no surprise. I seen her last month, looked like she was bout to die, head all cocked to the side. Guess when the Lord calls us on home aint nuthin we can do but get off our fat ass and go.   John Henry? MmHmm, seen that one comin too.   Huh? Dont ask me how to pronounce it, ask that damn dictionary.

Thats right, O-bit-u-ary.   Why you gone ask me when you got the dictionary in your hand. What you think it mean. You readin a list of dead folks and the title is Obiturary. Think for yaself cuz aint nobody else gonna think for you. Get over here and peel these onions. Get the molasses out ya ass, boy, you slow as shit out of a constipated person. Put some salt of them neckbones and stir them beans so they wont stick. Okay now, get back over there and see what that word mean.

I dont give a damn what you dont wanna do. You need to learn to read good cuz I dont want you sweepin white folks floors like I had to. I done raised so my many white chaps, taughtem how to clean up after theyself, taughtem some manners. Them kids couldnt pour piss out of a boot if it had a hole in the toe and instructions on the heel. But nobody ever said thanks, specially them white women, talk to you any kinda way, but let you clean they childrens ass. Who else done died, boy.

USUAL ROUTE

We hop on the trash truck and start collecting before the
sun fully rises. In the alley a bloody-mouthed raccoon gnaws
on a white baby shoe. It stands on a mattress with piss stains.
A yellow blob of chicken fat traced by a trail of ants. The
chicken fat slugs along a mucus path. A batch of flies pile on
the exposed red tendons and bone of a deer leg severed at
the knee. Three rat-like kittens moan like babies in a soggy
cardboard box. The fourth kitten is silent. Only the head
remains. Its deflated body lies shredded on the other end
of the mattress. Draped across the tops of three trash cans
are large bouquets of funeral flowers, wilted off-white and
droopy pink roses buried in full deep green leaves. The sun
peeks over the mountains, rays poking through fog, tinting
everything soft yellow.

JIVE-ASS CHUMPS

My grandad finally teaches me his card tricks. He says to act kinda dumb while doing the tricks to make them chumps think they are smart. He says not to show anybody his tricks. I won't, I promise. Ohh, I say, thats how you do it. Practice a lot first, he says, And once you get it down, you can always win some scratch off these suckas. → win

I practiced for a few weeks. Now I try it at school, I know who the suckas are cuz they're always talking about how much money they got. I start just like Grandad said by drinking before school and acting drunker than I really am. A ghost told me I could read minds, I say. I go through the motions, shuffling, fumbling the cards, messing up. I get to the end of the trick and slur, I bet you the next card I flip over is your card. No it aint, nigga, the sucka says, ya drunk ass dont know shit, I betcha fifty dollars. And of course, I flip the card, but it's not the card he thought I was gonna flip, so he owes me. Pay up, goddammit. But I aint got it on me right now. Gimme what you got then. I only got money for lunch, five dollars. I thought you was rich, nigga, give it here, you gonna be one hungry muthafucka today.

win # Gt Scrad by doing Card tricks

52

TELL YOU A STORY

Grandad is shuffling his cards at the kitchen table. Counting money. Shuffling more. Come here for a sec, he says to me. Lemme tell you a story. I sit next to him. What do you want, he says. You said you wanted to tell me a story, I say. Nope, he says, I said I wanted to tell You a story. Is your name You. No, I say. He busts out laughing. I been lookin for that muthafucka all my goddamn life, he says, if you ever find You, let me know.

Wants to tell You a
Story (someone named You)

PEOPLE'S INSTINCTIVE TRAVELS AND THE PATHS OF RHYTHM

Every night, me, my mom, and my sister walk around to our house to get our clothes for school the next day. Our little sister keeps her clothes at my stepdad's mama's house, the house we kind of live in. Mama, I say, why cant we move back to our old house. She doesn't say anything. We keep walking up the long hill. I'm kicking a rock. My sister says, Yeah, why cant we.

We walk in our house. Dog shit smells from the basement. We cover our noses. Make sure you come round here this weekend and clean this shit up, my mom says. Our dog Snow White was our little sister's birthday gift. Now she lives in the basement. I place a bowl of food at the top of the steps. I walk her every few weeks. That's also when I clean the basement. I scrape up shovels and shovels full of dog shit and toss them over the hill. Most piles are hard with fuzzy white hair. Some are fresh. Puddles of piss. Piss fossils, crusted yellow around edges of filmy pools. Brown vomit spots. She eats her own shit. When I walk Snow White I take her deep into the woods. I take off the leash and tell her to leave. I always see wild dogs, Go live with them. She starts to leave but comes back. I kicked her once, Leave stupid dog. I'm sorry.

My mom goes to her bedroom and shuts the door. She thinks we can't hear her crying. My sister is in our bedroom trying to choose between blue jeans and a skirt. She holds them up for me to see. Jeans, I say. Thanks, she says, then I'll wear the skirt. I look at my basketball and baseball trophies, dusty. My

54

Etch-A-Sketch, dusty. My sister's My Little Ponies, dusty. We went on a field trip to this museum of this famous family's house, I think the Hatfields, or the McCoys. The family died a long time ago. Their kitchen table was set up like they were about to have dinner. Their beds were made. And they had clothes hanging on the clothesline in the yard. That museum looks like our house but not dusty.

My mom comes out of her room, eyes red, coughing. Alright, lets go, she says. Can we stay here tonight, my sister says. I said lets go. We start walking, no one is talking. I'm kicking a rock. My mom's friend Solomon is sitting on his porch smoking a cigarette. He smokes long fancy cigarettes with a long black plastic holder. Heeey girl, he says to my mom, what yall doing tonight. Nothing honeychild, my mom says, just gettin some fresh air. Girl I know thats right, he says, You still cookin for them kids at that school. You know it, she says, thats the only time some of them kids get to eat. Some of them come in there lookin a hot mess too, they parents aint payin no attention to em. Well girl, Solomon says, I'm glad they got somebody like you down there, bless your heart. Alright, she says, take it easy Solomon, you be good now.

Solomon has to be good, everybody is watching him. Supposedly Donovan missed school because Solomon kidnapped him and tied him to a tree. That's what Donovan said, then he escaped by the skin of his teeth or something. They believed it because one day when Donovan had on a pink suit for church, Solomon called Donovan his cute little Easter bunny. We knew he always had eyes for Donovan, they said, keep your kids away from that faggot.

55

Bye Solomon, I say, Oh, I got some new drawings. Show em to me tomorrow, he says, See you later my cute little buddy. My sister says, Bye Solomon. See you later too my cute little girl.

We get to the house and my stepdad says to my mom, What took you so goddamn long. Nothing, she says, I was just down the street talking to Solomon. Aww hell, he says, that faggot aint got nothing to talk about.

My sister goes to take a bath. I go outside to take a drink of moonshine and smoke. Cardboard. With the little wavy holes. Like smoking a harmonica. When I come back it is my turn to bathe. My stepdad's mom, well, I call her grandma now. She doesn't like the water bill to be too high. So we all use the same bathwater. My little sister goes first, LaShawn next, Jamar after that, then my sister. I'm last.

I stick my toe in the cold grey. I'm not supposed to run new water into the tub but I have a trick. I wrap my washrag around the faucet and turn the knob just a little. Hot water slides down the front of the tub. The thick black ring around the tub is perfect for drawing. With my finger I draw a landscape from the back to the front, mountains and a train and a city and a sun and birds and trees. To make leaves I put my finger in the washrag and stipple around the branches. Grey soapsuds for people's afros. With my fingernail I scrape white off the bar of soap to highlight the trees and black clouds.

By the time I get out the tub everyone is asleep. I tip toe into the kitchen and creep open the refrigerator and pull out the jar of grape jelly and a bottle of applesauce. From

eating alone, everyone asleep

the cabinet I take out Oreos and two cans of potted meat. I sit on the stairs in the dark and eat half the jar of jelly, half the applesauce. A whole row of Oreos. Both cans of potted meat. I lay on the floor next to my sister. She is snoring. In between snores she says, Fuck you. . . kiss my ass . . . please dont. I shake her. Whats wrong, she says. Nothing, youre snoring too loud. I try to go to sleep but can't. I lie there thinking about my moonshine. The smell the taste the burning spot in the middle of my forehead when I drink it too fast. I creep outside to the back of the house, pull my moonshine from under the scrap wood, unscrew the lid, breath deep the scent, pour it down my throat. The middle of my forehead burns. I look up on the hill and Lisa's bedroom light is on. That's my sign, I think.

drinks cuz can't be... can't sleep

I walk up the backside of the hill to get to Lisa's house, pushing the weeds out the way, slipping on wet grass. I walk up the other hill by her window and knock. She lets me in, I was wondering if you was coming, didnt you see my light. Yeah, I had to do some stuff. Well I'm glad youre here now cuz its been itching and need a good licking. Lisa is older than me and is about to graduate so she is teaching me. She takes her panties off and pulls up her nightgown and pushes my head down. She lays on the bed and spreads her legs. Right there, she says, thats it.

goes to Lisa's house

I've been licking for a long time. That thing that connects my tongue to my mouth hurts. Can I put it in, I say. Keep licking, she says, just keep licking. Just let me put the tip in, I say, please. Maybe one day. You always say that. You wouldnt even know what to do, she says, this is only for older dudes who know how to work it. I wipe my mouth with my forearm and climb back through the window, it is

57

throbbing. I lay on her roof and unzip my pants. The moon is bright white. I wipe my hand on the rough shingles. Stumble back down the hill to the house. One more drink of shine. Go to sleep.

In the morning at the bus stop me and Leonard and Dee meet to go over the raps we were supposed to write yesterday. Leonard says to me, Man you look tired as shit. Dee says, yeah. Yeah, I say, I was up all night fucking Lisa. Man, you lucky as hell, man, Leonard says. Dont tell nobody, I say, we keeping it on the down low. No doubt, no doubt, says Dee. What do it feel like, Leonard says. Its hard to explain man, I say, it just feels good. No doubt, no doubt, says Dee. Anyway, I say, lets get to the raps. Lets just read our favorite lines then go over the rest at lunch.

Dee goes first, I'm magnificent, kickin this, ridiculous…ness, muthafuckas cant get with this…diss. Me and Leonard say, Oooh, that shit was tight.

Leonard goes, The names Leonard, but call me Leonardo, like Da Vinci, when I'm with a girl she says, pinch me, cuz she think she dreamin, and I'm schemin. Me and Dee say, Oooh, that shit was tight.

I go, I rap like Reynolds … um, if theres any assailants trying to assail me, Imma call the cops and theyre gonna need bail, G. Leonard and Dee say, What the fuck was that. I couldnt find a word to rhyme with Reynolds, but other than that whats wrong. I found assailants in the dictionary. Yalls shit was good, but if we're gonna be part of A Tribe Called Quest we gotta start using big words. Nigga you act like you was deep in the dictionary studying, Dee says, your lazy ass found a word in the A section. You couldve at least flipped to the Ps or some shit, like I did, perplexed on a perpendicular plane of paradoxes.

Read another, Leonard says, cuz that shit was weak. Okay, I say, Notice my use of similes and metaphors, you finally met a whore, and think you a mack, I stack, money like Pringles, hundreds not singles. Leonard and Dee say, Oooh, that shit was tight. But where was the big words. It was coming up, I say, yall aint give me time to get to it. Here it is, I bomb the nation with my diminutive conglomeration. Conglomeration aint no big word, Dee says, we learned that shit in English last week, thats a normal every day word. Never mind, I say. Wasnt the song we was writing for supposed to be called Back To Africa, Dee says, none of that shit had nothing to do with Africa. Leonard says, I dont know about yall, but I know Imma get some box in Africa, like Buck say, some of that jungle pussy.

Before we get on the bus I pour out half a can of Sprite. Whatchu doing that for, Dee says. Just wait, I say. We get on the bus and walk to the back. Check this out, I say opening my book bag, my aunts always leave Bacardi so I snuck it out the house. I pour it into the can of Sprite and hand it to Leonard. He drinks, hands it to Dee, back to me. I'm still thinking, I say, but I cant come up with a word that rhymes with Reynolds.

In homeroom Redneck Dana leans over with her cigarette breath and bits of dip in her teeth and says, Hey yall, I got some speed. Meet me in the stairwell after class. What is speed, I say. Its these lil pills, she says, that keep you awake all goddamn day. I got some Barcardi, I say. Hell yeah, buddy, she says, we gonna get fucked up today. Fuck this pussy ass school, and these fuckin dick lickin sons of bitches.

Me, Leonard, Dee, and Redneck Dana walk to the stairwell on the bottom floor in the old building that got shut down. They keep old music equipment down here. From the inside pocket of her jacket she pulls out a baggie full of white pills. I stole these from my uncle. She puts three on her tongue and drinks Bacardi to swallow. Whoo, thats some good shit right there. Dee does the same with two pills. So does Leonard. I'm sleepy as shit, I say, I probably need about five or six. Hell yeah, buddy, Dana says, that motherfucker knows how to do it. We leave, Dana plunges a fresh wad of dip in her lip.

Halfway through first period the walls start to bend and my mouth drips into my lap. I see a baby swimming in piss. My heart pumps inside my mouth. My dick thumps against my thigh. My head swells into a hot air balloon. Fire pooling in my throat. The baby is swimming inside the hot air balloon filled with piss. My teacher says she bombs the nation with her conglomeration. All I can do is draw. Draw. Just look out the window and draw the courthouse below, every detail, next to the courthouse the jailhouse, even the jailbirds on the playground, even the real birds on the barbed wire, the streets, streetlights, stop signs. Draw. Draw. I stand and float out of class. Leonard vomits in the hall in front of the lockers. I laugh, the corners of my mouth touch my eyes. I walk by Dana's class and nod. She flies out. What the fuck did you give me. I told you what I gave you. Dana, I never noticed before, but you are one sexy bitch. And you are one sexy chocolate motherfucker, lets go back down to the stairwell. We hold hands and float. Dana squeezes my ass. I squeeze hers. Kiss me. I stick my tongue in her mouth. Taste her menthol dip. Palm her titties. Suck them. I do. She unzips my pants, grabs my dick and yanks. Stick your fingers in me. I do. My voice leaks through my fingertips.

3. ENJOY CONTENTS

GILL SCOTT HERON, HOME IS WHERE, LOSE A TURN, BIOLOGY, FRUITY PEBBLES, WATER, SEVEN YARD LINE, TOUCHDOWN, PLOT, NEWS, WIN, BLUEPRINTS, HER, FLOOR PLANS, JUST THINK ABOUT IT, RERUN, OKAY, REN-DEZVOUS, OH, ALMOST, DISCO, STAY, STAY, STAY, STAY

GIL SCOTT HERON

I am digging through my uncle's closet to find clothes. I
like his seventies clothes, he doesn't wear them. I find a dark
brown leather jacket, reversible, light brown suede on the
other side. In the back of the closet underneath folded bell-
bottoms are two milk crates filled with records. I pull one
out. On it is only a man's head with an afro, 1971, Pieces of a
Man. What is a piece of a man. I put it on the record player
and the deep voice starts a poem about a revolution that will
not be televised. I've heard my uncles say this a lot. I let it
play while I dig for more clothes. Then this one song comes
on, he is howling:

Home is where the hatred is
Home is filled with pain, and it
Might not be such a bad idea
Might not be such a bad idea if I never
Never went home again.

I run to the record player and stare at the center of it with
my mouth open throat thumping. I yank the needle up.
Look around to make sure no one is looking and place the
needle back into the groove, watching the words in the center of the record spin.

Once the song is over I put the needle back to that track
and let the song spin again. Take the record off and trace
my finger along its edge. I look into the man's eyes, where is
your home. I slide the record back into its sleeve and wrap it
in an old tee shirt and place it on the top shelf in the closet,
stack jeans on top of it, camouflage. It is mine now.

finds
lots
of
old
things

plays
a
record

I pack my found clothes in my book bag and start walking back to the house. The gnats and moths are fluttering around the streetlight. The lightning bugs are blinking in the black. My mouth opens to sing but the words are lodged in my chest.

HOME IS WHERE

I peek from the slit
between my forearms.
Them. They come.
Eyes in all the heads glow.
The glow
melts my arm flesh.
Burgundy vessels drip
from bone.

↗ FG II

The graveyard this time of year is nice. Damp orange yellow
red leaves pile at headstones for pillows. Place my head in
leaves. Soil moist and black like chocolate cake and taste
like worms. Arms spread legs spread wind crawls up my
pants leg to pocket soft backs of knees. Slightly arched back
anchors shoulders to throat, jaw, head. Eyes fixed to the
blue grey. Meanwhile. An old deer limps over, sits like a
dog, licks my soles.

laying in graveyard

LOSE A TURN

Grandma thinks I'm her husband again. He died before I was born. She says to me, Remember when you came home from the mines all dirty and took me dancin. Yeah, I say, we had big fun. And that one gal, she says, whats her name, you know, that slew-footed heffa, the one starin at you. Aw cmon now, I say, that was nuthin, you know I only got eyes for you.

Grandma slips back in. She says, Boy, you wash them dishes yet. I was just about to, I say. Well what you waitin on. She changes the channel to Wheel of Fortune and solves a puzzle before I do, and before the people on the show do. Them some slow-ass folks on that show, she says. A commercial comes on. She looks at me, That was a real nice date, huh, dontcha remember.

I wasnt dirty I tell you that. I got off of work, came home, cleant myself up, and put on one of them nice suits, a real nice one. I told her to put on her dancin shoes cuz we was gonna hit the town. Now I aint never been the dancin type, but after I had me a few whiskies I shonuff cut a rug that night. I got to twirlin her round with one finger. Beige dress flutterin all over the place, showin them pretty legs. Boy I tell ya, that was a good night.

Grandma is too old to wipe her own butt. Last week when I was wiping her butt, she slipped out again. Who the fuck are you touchin my ass, she said. Like usual I was holding her arms with one hand while wiping her with the other. She started hitting me and trying to roll off her potty chair. My hand slipped down and shit smeared my forearm. Get the fuck off me, she said. The best thing to do is wait until she slips back, so I walked to bathroom to wash my arm and hand. I walked back to the room and she was still sitting on the potty chair. Its you again, she said, dear God, please help.

I told you we was gonna find a nice church in West Virginia once we got settled. I know the churches aint like the ones back home in Louisiana, but theyll do, baby. The mines payin me good, you makin some good friends, plus we got all these damn kids runnin round here. We gonna be alright.

Grandma finally called for me. I walked into the room and she said, Would you mind helping me please, I had a little accident. I started wiping her, but the shit had dried a little and the toilet paper kept crumbling off. I soaked a washrag with warm water and soap. Thank you, she said, it must be something I'm eating thats making me mess all over myself. She farted. And started laughing. Thats enough gas to put in that car out there, she said.

Wheel of Fortune comes back from commercial. After every plate I wash I turn and look at Grandma. As long as I can see her looking up like she is thinking I think she is present. As long as I can hear her calling out an R or S or T or L or N or E, I think she is present. Buy a vowel, she says. She's still here. Buy another vowel, she says. She's still here. Buy me some baking soda.

Now I'm her oldest daughter. They ran out of baking soda, I say. I dont care, she says, you gotta go to that store outside the coal camp, see if they got some. Okay, I say. She gives me some money and I walk outside. Might as well take a few sips of moonshine while I'm waiting. I'll keep the money so I can buy cigarettes tomorrow. Last week she made a mistake when she sent me/her daughter to the store and gave us a fifty-dollar bill. The next day I bought three bottles of E&J.

These scrips aint worth a damn, theyre only worth something on this coal camp. The stores outside the camp will take these scrips sometimes, but theyre only worth about half of real money, if that. I can see if the stores on the camp had everything you need, but they never have shit. They pay me this play money and I gotta put it right back in the company store. Pretty much workin for free. Kennedy should of stayed his ass down here when he came campainin back in 60, talkin bout a war on poverty. War on shit.

I walk back in. Can you come over here and comb my hair for the night, she says, and dont forget to grease my scalp. I don't know if I'm still her oldest daughter or myself because I've combed Grandma's hair as her oldest daughter and as myself. Stop combing my hair like I'm a doll, she says, I aint that tender-headed. Okay, that means I'm myself because she always tells me that.

I part her hair down the middle. She usually dyes it but the gray is taking over. I slip my finger in the hair grease and slide it down the part. Jamar comes in from hanging out with his friends. Where you been, she says. I was out, Jamar says. Well since youre back, she says, mop this damn floor like I told you yesterday. I aint doing shit, he says. She pulls out her twenty-two from her purse in her lap and shoots at the wall next to Jamar. Crazy ass woman, he says grabbing the mop and bucket. I don't know if this is now-her, or then-her, because I guess she has always shot at people. My stepdad and his sisters said she's had that pistol for a long time and used to shoot at people for coming in her house. Said she didn't like living so close to people on the coal camp because they thought should share everything, even each other.

My stepdad pulls up and busts in the house, tracking mud on the wet floor that Jamar just mopped. I know why he's mad. Earlier I stole his three joints from underneath his car seat. He doesn't want his mama to know he smokes weed, so he stomps in yelling, Who stole my goddamn cigarettes. He looks at me and Jamar. I knew it was one of you morons. Who did it. Which one of you muthafuckas took my god-damn cigarettes. Grandma looks up and says, When did you start smoking cigarettes. He doesn't say anything. He goes to the living room and starts watching teevee, mumbling, stole my cigarettes.

LaShawn slips in the house and goes straight to Grandma's room and turns on the teevee. I don't know where she was, maybe with her boyfriend. My mom walks in carrying pizza boxes from her second job at Lil Caesar's in the new Kmart that just opened. She says hello to my Grandma and yells in the living room to my stepdad, You got any cigarettes left.

When we gonna take a trip back down to Louisiana, Grandma says. *Well I dont know, depends.* Depends on what. *Um, depends on how much time I can get off work, and depends on whether or not we gotta take all these kids, cuz I hate these fuckers, especially my stepdad,* I say. Damn, I slipped up. I hope she slips back in. Your stepdad, Grandma says, yeah, no need to take him with us. *Just me and you, Chicken, just me and you.* That sounds nice, she says, just like that trip we took up to Cleveland to see your brother. Damn, she's never mentioned a trip to Cleveland before. *Yeah,* I say, *that was a cool trip.*

Good ol Cleveland, love that place, especially the Indians. Did we go to a baseball game, Chicken. Naw, dont remember no baseball game.

Cleveland? We aint never been to no damn Cleveland. We visited some kin folk up in New York and D.C., even made it out west to St. Louis. Got on the Greyhound and went to see my cousins, only had two kids then.

I switch to her oldest daughter because I can't remember anything about Cleveland. While I'm putting rollers in her hair I say, Mhm girl, we gotta do something about these split ends. Boy, why you talkin like a faggot, she says. We clear our throat.

My sister and my little sister come in from playing outside. My little sister tells my sister, He aint your real daddy anyway. My sister says, Like I give a fuck. Ooh, I'm tellin, says my little sister. She goes to the living room with my mom and stepdad. My sister says to me, You need some help, youre terrible at rolling hair. Thanks, I say, and give her the rollers and hair grease. Before I walk away, Grandma smacks my hand and says, Didnt I tell your little fat ass to do your homework. Now she thinks I'm my stepdad. She can think whatever the fuck she wants. I am not acting like my stepdad.

72

BIOLOGY

Merna is popular because she gives head to a lot of dudes. Last night at the football game she gave Buck head under the bleachers. She has a cute birthmark on her cheek close to her lips. Buck says, You know how people get birthmarks, right. No, I say. People get birthmarks when theyre in the moms belly, and when the dad is fucking the mom the tip of his dick hits the baby. So, he says, shes used to sucking dick cuz she been doing it for so long. And I know you want her to be your girlfriend, but you should never date a girl with a birthmark on her mouth.

What happens
at bleachers
during Football
games

FRUITY PEBBLES

My cousin leaves me in charge. He says, I gotta make a run and will be back tonight. Just give em what they need. Marissa probably gonna come through. She'll wanna suck your dick, but dont give that broad shit unless she pay. I made that mistake a few times. She do got some good head though.

I sit on the couch eating Fruity Pebbles and watching Tom & Jerry. Make sure the thirty-eight on the coffee table is loaded. Someone knocks on the door. I grab the gun and peek out the curtain before I open it. It's crazy Percy, Lemme get a couple rocks. You got money. He shows it to me. Be right back.

I finish my cereal while Tom still chases Jerry. Someone knocks. Grab the gun and peek out. It's Marissa. Her baby is crying in its stroller and the other one is crying on her hip. Lemme get a rock. You got money. No, my check dont come till next week. Well, come back next week. I'll suck your dick. Umm, maybe, nah. Please, pretty please, just one rock, a half of rock. Come back when you got some fuckin money. Please. No, Marissa. She walks away saying, Fuck you then, nigga. Nobody dont wanna suck your lil dick anyway, ole hoe-ass nigga.

Tom still chases Jerry. Someone knocks. Grab gun and peek. It's my football coach. What the fuck you doing here, he says. What the fuck you doing here, I say. Minding my fuckin business, where ya cousin at. I'm taking care of shit today. Well, lemme get a couple eight balls. A couple, what are you gonna do with a couple. Look muthafucka, you gonna give em to me or not. You got money. Of course I got money, who the fuck you think I am. Okay man, chill the fuck out, be right back. I give him the eight balls and look outside. Marissa is peeking around the corner of the house next door with the roof caved in. The stroller wheels are sticking out. I yell, No, Marissa. She yells back, Please. My coach yells, I gotcha baby, dont worry bout this lil snot-nosed nigga. They walk inside the house.

Later my cousin comes home. I tell him who bought what and that I didn't get my dick sucked no matter how much I wanted to. I hand him the money. He says, Keep it all, you did good. Its hard not to let that bitch suck your dick. Matter of fact, I might call her back over here and let her top me off.

The next day at practice I tackled our quarterback when I shouldn't have. He said something about my mom being on welfare so after he was on the ground I put him in a head-lock and spit in his fucking face. My coach runs over yelling, I done told you, muthafucka. Run ten laps. Yeah right, I say, fuck you.

WATER

My cousin buys a house. He says, Niggas dont know what do with they dope money, real estate is where its at. These white folks been flippin it for years. I tell him his house is nice. Fuck a nice, he says, its about location. Oh, I say, because you bought it next to white folks. Kinda, he says, but not really. Just listen, its about location, physical in this case, not social or economic. Huh, I say.

Pay attention lil cuz, this house is way up at the top of this hill. Now, he says polishing his hot dog cart in front of the new house, in the unfortunate event of a residential fire, it is the citys responsibility to extinguish said fire. These white folks done fucked up and put the closest hydrant way at the bottom. You prolly thinking the fire truck can just roll up here and put the fire out. Yeah, I say, the fire truck can just roll up here and put the fire out. Wrong, he says.

See, Imma wait till winter when we get a good snow. Then Imma hose this street down, straight ice. These old white folks go to sleep at six so they wont see shit. Once that truck cant get up here, they gonna try to hook up to that hydrant. Wont they have hoses that connect, I say. Fuck no, he says, the average length of a fire hose is about fifty feet, and these trucks in this lil ass town only carry about five hoses. Do some math real quick nigga, fifty times five. Umm, I say. Too slow, nigga, I know you good at math cuz I taught you, two hundred and fifty. Yeah, I say, thats right, two hundred and fifty.

From the hydrant to this house is a half a mile, how many feet is that. A mile, I say, is five thousand two hundred and eighty feet, divided by two—Too slow nigga, two thousand six hundred and forty. Yeah, I say, thats right.

I only spent thirty grand on this house. Put in hardwood floors for two grand. All I paid for was material cuz crazy Percy do labor for a few rocks. Got a new big screen, all that shit. Got new beds for the kids. I made copies of all the pictures from mom's photo album and put em in a new one. Gotta have some priceless sentimental shit. Basically, it shows I care about this fuckin house. Imma sue the city for way more than I invested. I got home insurance, car insurance, I even got insurance on this hot dog stand. All this shit is gonna burn to the ground by the time the fire department get up here. If they get up here.

It is February. Earlier I scraped ice off the church steps because we are having an anniversary service for Pastor Johnson tonight. My cousin sits next to me reading Psalms 23. He points to, My cup runneth over. Pastor Johnson is thanking the congregation for a lovely turnout. Miss Hattie went outside for a cigarette a few minutes ago because she was nodding off. She bust back in the church, cigarette in hand, and runs to my cousin, Your house is on fire. Everyone gasps. My aunt says, Put out that goddamn cigarette. My cousin grabs his coat and runs out. We stand on the church steps and look up on the hill. My cousin's house against the snow looks like the candles burning on the white tablecloth in the pulpit.

The next day I see my cousin. You shoulda seen it, he says, that fire truck was just a spinnin.

SEVEN YARD LINE

I fucking hate Terrell. He's always talking shit about my clothes, my mom, my fat stepdad, my sister, everything. Every fucking day. Imma get his ass, somehow.

He's a senior and the football star so everybody kisses his ass and the teachers let him skip class and they still give him good grades. But he's dumb as fuck, can't even read aloud in class. What the fuck is he doing in sophomore English anyway. I can't make fun of him for being dumb because nobody cares. What else.

Last year his older brother was playing with a gun and accidentally shot himself in the face. At the funeral Terrell and his friends sang a song called Gangsta Lean. Gangsta Lean is about these dudes' homie who got shot in the hood or something. In the song they tell god to tell their dead homie to stop shooting dice in heaven so he can hear them sing. And they pour out forties and sing about their gangsta memories. Terrell was crying like a bitch. That's it! I can fuck with him for crying. No, you can't make fun of somebody for crying at a funeral. Fuck.

The next day at football practice while we walk onto the field Terrell says his usual dumb shit, Thats why ya mama on welfare. Shut the fuck up, I say. (Fuck, that was weak.) Aww, is the welfare baby mad, look at those cheap ass shoes, you crooked teeth motherfucker. Everyone laughs, Terrell you wild as hell man, you always have me rolling. Oh you think thats funny, I say, You know what I think is funny. (What do I think is funny, think, think.) What, crack baby, he says, What the fuck do you think is funny. Um, I say, I think its

78

funny that you sung Gangsta Lean when your stupid-ass brother shot himself, there is nothing gangsta about that, oops, I blew my stupid brains out.

Terrell slams his helmet into my mouth. One of his friends tackles me. Another one pulls my shirt over my head and they start kicking me in the ribs. Stomping on my back, cleats digging in my skin. You went too far motherfucker. I'm swallowing blood. Kicking, stomping, until I hear our coach yelling stop goddammit stop.

Terral's reaction ♩
(Rears him up)

TOUCHDOWN

My art teacher really likes my stuff. She arranges for me to have an art show for a week at the public library. Pencil drawings of the courthouse and watercolor wolves howling and oil waterfalls I copied from Bob Ross and acrylic trains with graffiti and pastel dogs and ink house in winter forest. I tell everybody in town, at school, home, church: Guess what, my show opens after school on Friday before my football game at seven-thirty.

My teacher says to meet her there immediately after school. People love to meet the artist, she says. I wear my uncle's brown leather jacket and my white polyester shirt with the butterfly collar. After I iron my jeans I polish my brown boots. Splash cologne, Cool Water.

I stand in front of the watercolor wolves wiping my sweaty palms on my pants. My sister walks in smiling. Hey Mister Arteest, she says. How did you get down here, I say, dont you supposed to be at home. I missed the bus on purpose and caught a ride, she says. She puts her face close to the wolves and squints, goes to another picture, squints. You've already seen these, I say. So, she says.

An hour passes. No one comes. Another hour. Still no one. Let's go smoke I tell my sister. We stand outside shivering, passing a Black & Mild, smoke mixing with the steam from our breath. Well, I say, its time for me to go the game.

Everyone is at the game, cheering and cussing out the refs and carrying on like at every game. I get a sack and catch a couple of passes and get an interception. I don't know the

80

score but we win. It was a scrubby team. After the game people give me high-fives. My stepdad smacks my helmet and
tells me I did a great job and that I really showed that other
team. That's my boy, he says to the man next to him.

Every day the next week my sister misses the bus and goes
to the library with me. I skip football practice. No one ever
comes. Me and my sister shiver while we smoke a Black
& Mild. I draw a picture of her with a big cloud of smoke
floating from her mouth and hang it next to the watercolor
wolves.

Wants to show people art, no one comes

PLOT

Miss Janice died this morning. She fell asleep and crashed her car into the creek. They don't know if she drowned or died on impact. Mr. Ray died yesterday. He just died. The day before yesterday Malik died. He was driving and fell and asleep and got hit by a semi. Lord I tell ya, Grandma says, Death happens in threes.

Does she mean only people. Only people we know, or people in general. If it's people we know she might be wrong because Aunt Ruth died last Friday. I want to die on impact. If she means people in general, that might be wrong too because all those people just died at that school in Colorado. I think the news said 12, or 21. Either way, 12 and 21 are multiples of 3.

If death happens in multiples that means it can form a linear line. I plotted death on a graph by putting death in a linear equation as y. (y =2x +1) When x increases, y increases twice as fast. But this equation does not include time, how death happens, death in other places, stranger death, death type. There are too many unknown variables. For now, the best I can come up with is Death = x. And x = ∞. A kicked over 8. Death happens in a kicked over 8.

NEWS

Harold Muncy, Jr. was born on December 6, 1937 and passed away December 1, 1997. Harold was a resident of Chikataw, West Virginia at the time of his passing.

It is with great sadness that the family of Wilma Simpson announces her passing, after a long battle with cancer at the age of 65 years. Born in Lowerville, she was the daughter of the late William Simpson and Eula Mae Simpson.

Obituaries

Gabriel Ray Mason, infant son of Mark Mason and Brandy Mason, departed this life Saturday at Thornfield Community Hospital. Memorial services will be held at Trinity Baptist Church, where he was a member.

I crossed out my grandad's description. It was stupid.

WIN

Our football coach tells me, Leonard, and Dee that we are a waste of space on the team. He's right. But he's mad because we are losing by forty points at half-time so he starts giving a speech saying we could come back and win but Dee busts out laughing and slapping his knees. Then me and Leonard start laughing at Dee. Everyone looks at us, This is important to us, shut the fuck up. They believe the coach about coming back to win.

After halftime we are standing on the sideline and Leonard talks about how hard the dirt is because of the cold. You think this is something, I say, you should see the permafrost up in the tundra. Dee says, It is colder than a muthafucka out here. Wait, I have an idea. Dee tells us his idea. Me and Leonard agree.

The clock is counting down to the end of the fourth quarter. We are losing sixty to zero. Five, four, three, two, one . . . Me, Leonard, Dee grab the water cooler and dump it on our coach's head. Ice bounces off his shoulders to the ground. Yay, congratulations, coach.

BLUEPRINTS

Me, Leonard, and Dee signed up for vocational school. Drafting. It's the best because its drawing and math combined. We do all types of shit. Designing cabinets for the construction department. Designing bolts and precision tools for the welding department. Sometimes we use a computer program called Autocad to render 3-D objects and reduce the amount of calculated error from hand-drawn designs. We even learned how to survey land. We surveyed the football field for the county so a new sewer pipe could be ran underneath. The paperwork has our names on it: Surveyed by Me, Leonard, and Dee. Nobody will ever see it because it's in the courthouse records. My favorite though, is when we design floor plans for houses.

Signs up for vocational
Class, explains what they
do

HER

There's this girl at school, younger than me, a sophomore. She is short and thin and wears all black, black nail polish black lipstick and short blond hair showing her soft neck. Thick soles on black boots buckle up to her calves. A long chain connects her front and back pockets. She does not smile or talk.

I always see her in the hall after class. I finally walk up and say hi. She looks, mouth closed, eyes narrowed, and says, What. I just wanted to say hi, I say. Hi, she says. Um, I say, I gotta go to my next class, do you mind if we talk more at lunch. I guess, she says. See you then, I say.

At lunch I walk to her table with my tray. I ask her name and where she's from. Laura, she says, Im from nowhere and everywhere. Cool, I say, How you like school. I dont, she says. Cool, I say. Um, I did just wanna say hi earlier, but another reason is . . . I bite my pizza. She bites hers. With my spoon I shovel the fruit cocktail into another compartment. The other reason is, I think youre pretty and I like your clothes. She looks at me, back down at her tray, back up at me, I like your clothes too, kinda seventies.

For the next few weeks we talk everyday at lunch. We decided that we're both cool and should go together. She even smiles. Especially when we make fun of her grandad and my grandma. Her mock deep voice says, What are you doing with that nigger. My mock high voice says, What you are doing with that white bitch. We raise our chocolate milk cartons, Cheers, white bitch. Cheers, nigger.

FLOOR PLANS

I am going to be an architect. A fucking architect. I will design my own house. In Japan. Or Norway. Or Spain. I will design my house with bonsai trees and a waterfall in the foyer. With the living room windows facing south. With frosted glass showers. I will design my house without eight people living in it. Without people yelling back and forth through the house. Without tevees blaring in every room. I bet you I'm gonna be an architect, godammit.

talks about how he'll design his house

JUST THINK ABOUT IT

My cousin joined the Navy. Every day at school he wears his blue and yellow Navy windbreaker and blue and yellow Navy ball cap. His recruiter comes to our school all the time and flirts with the girls and the boys all the time. The girls giggle and the boys' voices get deeper. They all like his white clothes and his little white hat and his black leather portfolio. My cousin and his recruiter stroll up to me at lunch. They ask have I thought about joining the Navy. They say I should join the Navy for my father god and my uncle Sam. Hell no, I say, what I look like fighting for the man. I'm going to college, jack.

RERUN

Last year before LaShawn graduated high school, my mom, stepdad, and grandma drove her around to lots of different colleges. Ohio, Tennessee, North Carolina, and a few here in West Virginia. LaShawn finally decided on a big university in Ohio. My mom wore the university sweatshirt around the house every day, put the university sticker on her car, and the university magnets on the refrigerator. She'd tell everyone in town, My girl went to that big university in Ohio, and shes doing real good up there too.

This year LaShawn is back home. She is taking a semester off because they said something happened to her at that big university in Ohio. In the morning she sits on the bed and takes a few white pills and eats bacon sandwiches while watching reruns of Saved By the Bell. When we come from school she is taking pills and eating bacon sandwiches and watching Saved By the Bell.

Because I'm about to graduate and want to go to college and because LaShawn is smart, I ask her how was college. She says, Zack Morris is funny.

My mom sits at the kitchen table. I unfold my map and point with my pen to three places I want to go to college. My pen lines connect the roads between our town to two towns in northern West Virginia, and one in Tennessee. I already did the research, I say, but I wanna visit University of Tennessee first because they have the best architecture program, its only three hours away. My mom looks at me, I dont know how you gonna get there.

OKAY

I joined the Navy. So did Leonard and Dee. We are supposed to leave together in August, on the Buddy Program,
where we're gonna be in boot camp together or something.

Me and my recruiter are trying to figure out my job in the
Navy. You scored an eighty one on your ASVAB, he says, so
you can pretty much pick whatever you want. Cool, I say.
Heres some nuclear stuff, he says, like working with bombs.
Cool, I say, sign me up. Oh never mind, he says, your physical says youre colorblind, so you cant work with nuclear stuff
in case you have to cut wires to diffuse a bomb.

He flips through the big binder. This is good, he says squint-
ing, cripe-crip-cryptological technician. Whats that, I say.
Basically its spy stuff, like real James Bond type shit. For
real, I say. Yeah, youll be wearing suits and stuff. Hell yeah,
I say, sign me up. Can I live in Spain as a spy, and get some
girls. Of course, he says, you can live anywhere you want,
plus, Spanish broads love American spies.

I guess this sounds good, I say, but I dont wanna be in no
wars. Let me put things in perspective for you, he says. The
last war was in the early nineties, before that was the seventies, and before that was the forties, thats about twenty to
thirty years between wars. Its ninety nine now, there wont be
another war until after long youre retired.

RENDEZVOUS

Me and Laura walk out of French class. One day, she says, we are going to hang out in Pah-ree at fucking chezzz fancy chef. Oui, we will, I say. I'll be living in Spain, so when I get a break from my spy stuff I'll meet you in Pah-ree. We grab each other's hand and start walking to lunch. Look, someone says, its J.J. from Good Times and Dracula's daughter. Then Shariqua yells, Niggas always fuckin with them white hoes.

What time should I come over tonight, I say. How about right after school, she says. Wont your folks be awake. Thats the point, she says, I was thinking you could come through the front door this time. What about your grandad. He doesnt get off work till six, she says, and you can leave by then. Plus I really want my grandma to meet you, I told you shes cool. I mean, she was a little hesitant at first, but I told her shit she wanted to hear, like you were a respectful young man and well dressed and got good grades, she was pretty surprised. She even thought you might be a good influence on me after I told her you went to church. Damn, I say, you should quit jiving that lady.

After school we get on the bus that goes to her neighborhood. We sit together and Laura tries to hold my hand but I keep wiping my palms on my corduroys. Dont tell me youre scared of a little old white lady, she says. We step off the bus, up the cobbled walk way between trimmed hedges to her front door. As Laura reaches to the crystal doorknob, the door swings open and her grandma waves us in, Oh hello darlings. How was school. So this is the mister, it is nice to finally meet you. Good evening, maam, I say, It is also nice to meet you.

We follow her into the dining room to a long wooden table already set. Yall just sit down now, she says. You have a beautiful house, I say, thank you for inviting me. Laura puts her hand on my thigh and smiles. Supper is just about ready, Grandma says, you kids go wash up.

She brings out roast beef and mashed potatoes and green beans. Laura has told me that youre quite the church goer, she says, would you mind saying the blessing. I would be honored, I say bowing my head, Heavenly Father, please bless this beautiful meal that will, um, nourish our bodies and our souls and um, please bless Mrs. White, who prepareth this meal before us. Amen.

So, Laura tells me youve decided to join the Navy after you graduate. Yes, I say, I have always wanted to serve our country. How wonderful, she says, we need more young men like you around here, Lord knows we could use them. Laura squeezes my thigh and smiles. And thats why I love him, grandmother.

I eat half of my food while we talk about school and more church. The front door opens. We stop chewing and look at each other confused. A man's voice says, Hello, I got off early, yall home. He walks into the dining room and when he sees me he stops. Turns around and walks back out. I think its time for me to go, I say. Oh no, honey, the grandma says, its fine, he probably had a bad day at work. I stand, he walks in again, What is he doing in my house. I snatch my backpack and walk around the table far from him and out the door. Laura runs out after me. He yells, I thought I raised you better than to be chasing some nigger out in the street.

92

I walk down the road a bit with my arm out and thumb up. The sheriff stops and picks me up as always. Youre leavin a little earlier than usual, he says, everything go alright. Yeah, I say, it was cool. I met her grandma, she's nice. I see, he says, I also saw the grandpa's truck out front, now I know you aint gonna say he's cool, cuz I know he aint cool. Yeah, I say, he aint cool. I know what youre thinking, he says, and not all us old white men hate black folks. Things a changing, he says, now I dont like all these lil hippy hoppy punks with they pants hangin off they ass, hell, I dont even like them lil white punks. I wasnt thinking that, I say. I'd think it if I was you. It aint the first time I've been called a nigger, I say. And it wont be the last, he says.

The next day at school Laura says, So, my grandma thinks 'very highly' of you. I bet, I say. So youre gonna be an asshole today, she says. I guess. Well, she says, I'm on punishment, cant go anywhere for two months. Really, I say. Yep, she says smiling, I showed him our prom pictures.

A few weeks ago I asked Laura what she thought about proms. Stupid, she said, cheesy as fuck, they all look the same, the proms and the people, all the stupid bitches wear too much make-up and dumb-ass shiny princess dresses. I feel the same, I said, but we should go anyway, just to get us both out, just to have a night where I dont have to sneak in your bedroom window. Yeah right, she said, like my folks would let me go the prom with a black dude. Already got it figured out, I said.

One of my friends is a white dude and he has a black girl-friend. They wanted to go to prom together, but you know.

So I told my friend that he should take Laura to the prom and I would take his girlfriend. Then we'd swap when we got to the prom. That's what we did. Laura and my friend took a nice white prom picture together to show to their folks. And me and my friend's girlfriend took a nice black picture together to show to our folks. Then we swapped and took pictures with our own girlfriends, to hide and keep to ourselves. My cousin let me borrow his car. He even paid to rent my tux.

Fake prom dates

We got to the prom. Laura said, I look stupid. She had on a shiny light blue dress because her grandma thought she looked cute. I looked like James Bond, white coat, black pants, black bow tie. We were at the prom for a little more than thirty minutes and got the fuck out of there. We went to a hotel, which my cousin gave me money for. We drank Wild Turkey and smoked Salems. Free as we wanted to be. It was a nice prom.

Yeah, Laura says, he flipped his shit when I showed him the pictures. Good job, I say. He wanted to make me transfer schools but Grandma wouldnt let him. She tried to stand up for you but he told her to shut the fuck up because none of that shit matters. Not to him, I say. I wish I was pregnant, she says. No you don't, I say. Fuck no I don't, she says, but it'll piss him the fuck off even more. I love you, she says. Love you too. So what do we do from here, she says. I have no fuckin idea. Youll probably forget about me anyway when you leave. And youll probably forget about me too when I leave. Maybe not, she says. Maybe not, I say.

94

OH

Me and my sister are at my aunt's house looking through her old photo albums. She talks about my grandad, her and my mom's dad, how he used to paint his fingernails with clear polish so his fingers would sparkle while he shuffled the cards. I sure miss my daddy, she says. At least you knew your daddy, I say. She looks at me, and sighs. Well, she says, I know you've asked your mama, and since she will never tell you I will.

My aunt closes the photo album and lights a cigarette, Your mama was young, real young, and stupid, hell both of em was stupid, her and your daddy. Anyway, ya mama had you first of course, and by then they had already been fighting, he was beating her, she was beating him, lord Jesus, all types of crazy stuff. Then ya mama got pregnant with your sister and her twin. They got to fightin again, your dad was drunk, or high, probably both. And while your mama was pregnant he pushed her out of a window. And thats what sent her into labor early, way early, too damn early. My aunt turns to my sister, You lived, and even though both you and your sister were in that incubator for a few months, she just didnt make it.

My aunt looks at me, Now you know, so stop giving your mama a hard time about it. Oh, and after yall were born your dad tried to kidnap you but your mama shot him in the leg and we aint seen him since, he might be dead somewhere for all I know.

ALMOST

He can hear the wind from the belt before it smacks his bare ass, he grabs the belt, a little sting, and swings his head around mouth tight, he starts to grow, tall wide solid but the voices come bigger and thicker than he is, flooding dark and stale, righting the wrong. He drops the belt, turns back around, and shrinks like he is supposed to.

about
story ?

DISCO

He walks into the house and into the living room and they are all dead. Slumped in sofas, heads down. He sees no marks on the bodies but blood coats the floor. A disco ball lowers from the ceiling and he starts break dancing, spinning on his back makes the blood paint the walls. He does a headstand, still spinning, legs in a split. He stands striking a pose, arms crossed, then moonwalks out the house. A black horse with armor and an afro clops to him and opens its mouth. He reaches inside and pulls out a blood-streaked Samurai sword. He back flips onto the horse's back and says, Giddy-up, god-dammit. The horse does not move.

STAY

It's yearbook signing time. There is a mixture of kinda excited and kinda not excited. Everyone at school is passing around their yearbooks. Writing stuff like, First to sign your crack, Have a great summer, These are the best years of our life. I hope not. A few people write in my yearbook, Stay crazy, Stay yourself, Stay nice. I look at the people under The Most Talented section, and they are. And under my photo in the The Most Talented section, someone writes, Stay talented. It's like everybody wants you to stay. That's why I don't write shit in nobody's yearbook.

STAY

After graduation everyone does this graduation thing where they stay at the school overnight and play games and try to sneak in empty classrooms to fuck. Instead I buy a bottle of Wild Turkey 101 and a pack of Newports and go sit on top of the hill in a cloud of lightning bugs. I think there is a pattern to their flashes, three seconds here, three there. Blinks of green and yellow in the black wrap around my cigarette smoke. After I drink half the bottle the mosquitoes stop biting but pods of skin still bubble up on my arms and neck. I see my sister slipping on the wet grass walking up the hill. She lights a cigarette and takes a swig and hands the bottle back to me. I take a swig, holding it in my mouth to keep the burn. She looks at me, smiles, and says, Congraduations. The bourbon spews out of my nose. She slaps her knee, I thought of that earlier today. She takes a drag, red glow, Well, I'll be by myself when you leave.

STAY

Over the summer, me, Leonard, and Dee run five miles every morning to get in shape for boot camp, even if we stayed up late getting fucked up. A few times a week we break into swimming pools at night, climbing over the fence, to teach Leonard how to swim. Twice this week I vomited before we ran. Hey man, Leonard says, dont you think you might be drinking too much. Fuck no, I say, I still come in first on these runs every goddamn day. Dont you think you drinking too much water when youre drowning in that pool. Whatever, he says.

What he did during Summer

STAY

I'm trying to fix the leaking pipes under the bathroom sink. My stepdad waited until today to tell me to fix them. Yesterday he wanted me to fix a leak in the roof. I still have tar on my hands my arms my face my neck my chest. It's hard to get that shit off. It feels like it will be on my body forever. I removed all the pipes under the sink, and when I am about to put them back, my recruiter pulls up and blows the horn. Leonard and Dee are already in the backseat. I start to walk out and I see my mom shuffling herself into position for a hug. I pat my pockets and look around like I forgot something. Once I'm outside my stepdad yells, You aint finish fixing this goddamn sink. My sister looks out the window upstairs and touches her eyebrow with two fingers. I nod. I get in the car, nod at Leonard and Dee. And my recruiter pulls off.

NOTES

"Heavy D" contains lyrics from "Now That We Found Love" by Heavy D & The Boyz. (Uptown Records, 1990)

"Confirmation" contains lyrics from "First of tha Month" by Bone Thugs-n-Harmony. (Ruthless Records, 1995)

"People's Instinctive Travels and the Paths of Rhythm" is the title of a A Tribe Called Quest album. (Jive Records, 1990)

"Gil Scott Heron" contains lyrics from "Home is Where the Hatred is" by Gil Scott-Heron. (Flying Dutchman, 1972)

"Seven Yard Line" contains lyrics from "Gangsta Lean" by D.R.S. (Roll Wit It Entertainment, 1993)

ACKNOWLEDGEMENTS

Tara Saulibio: An intelligent/sensitive reader and my wife, whose constant support and encouragement allows me the time, space, and energy to pursue writing. Tara, without you, I don't think I could do any of this.

Jada Dunn: My daughter, who at eleven-years-old, named the three sections of this book. Jada, I appreciate your creativity and willingness to read what I ask you to. And thank you for asking about my writing, and making sure I was writing.

Lorenzo James and Brian Lupo were generous and patient readers who felt every word and page for a few years, giving me insight on all levels, even when it came to arranging this book. Thank you so goddamn much!

Selah Saterstrom: Her classes, her writing, her advocacy and generosity, were so important in getting this book started and getting through it. She's the all-around shit, and I'm fortunate that our lives bumped into each other. Sometimes I feel like "thank you" isn't enough, so my "thank you" to Selah will be in the form of continuing to deepen my practice and being in service to the mysteries of reading and writing.

I am grateful for everyone who has read parts of this book, especially Felix Hamm, Anwar Belt, Paul Turner, Isaiah Baggett, Kevin Wright, and DeShawn Crawford. Y'all's conversations, questions, and open ears helped more than y'all realize.

Thanks also to the editors of *Columbia Journal* and *Tarpaulin Sky Magazine*, who published excerpts from this book.

ABOUT THE AUTHOR

Steven Dunn was born and raised in West Virginia, and after 10 years in the Navy he earned a B.A. in Creative Writing from University of Denver. He is the Reviews & Interviews Editor for Horse Less Press, and currently lives in Denver.

TARPAULIN SKY PRESS
Current Titles (2016)

hallucinatory ... trance-inducing (*Publishers Weekly* "**Best Summer Reads**"); warped from one world to another (*The Nation*); somewhere between Artaud and Lars Von Trier (*VICE*); simultaneously metaphysical and visceral ... scary, sexual, and intellectually disarming (*Huffington Post*); only becomes more surreal (*NPR Books*); horrifying and humbling in their imaginative precision (*The Rumpus*); wholly new (*Iowa Review*); breakneck prose harnesses the throbbing pulse of language itself (*Publishers Weekly*); the opposite of boring.... an ominous conflagration devouring the bland terrain of conventional realism (*Bookslut*); creating a zone where elegance and grace can gambol with the just-plain-fucked-up (*HTML Giant*); both devastating and uncomfortably enjoyable (*American Book Review*); consistently inventive (*TriQuarterly*); playful, experimental appeal (*Publishers Weekly*); a peculiar, personal music that is at once apart from and very much surrounded by the world (*Verse*); a world of wounded voices (*Hyperallergic*); dangerous language, a murderous kind.... discomfiting, filthy, hilarious, and ecstatic (*Bookslut*); dark, multivalent, genre-bending ... unrelenting, grotesque beauty (*Publishers Weekly*); futile, sad, and beautiful (*NewPages*); refreshingly eccentric (*The Review of Contemporary Fiction*); a kind of nut job's notebook (*Publishers Weekly*); thought-provoking, inspired and unexpected. Highly recommended (*After Ellen*).

Set in a decaying town in southern West Virginia, this debut novel
from Steven Dunn, *Potted Meat*, follows a young boy into adoles-
cence as he struggles with abusive parents, poverty, alcohol addic-
tion, and racial tensions. Using fragments as a narrative mode to
highlight the terror of ellipses, *Potted Meat* explores the fear, power,
and vulnerability of storytelling, and in doing so, investigates the
peculiar tensions of the body: How we seek to escape or remain em-
bodied during repeated trauma. "Steven Dunn's *Potted Meat* is full
of wonder and silence and beauty and strangeness and ugliness and
sadness and truth and hope. I am so happy it is in the world. This
book needs to be read" (**LAIRD HUNT**). "*Potted Meat* is an extraordinary book. Here is an emerging voice that calls us to attention. I
have no doubt that Steven Dunn's writing is here, like a visceral in-
tervention across the surface of language, simultaneously cutting to
its depths, to change the world. My first attempt at offering words
in this context was to write: thank you. And that is how I feel about
Steven Dunn's writing; I feel grateful: to be alive during the time in
which he writes books" (**SELAH SATERSTROM**).

Dana Green's debut collection of stories, *Sometimes the Air in the Room Goes Missing*, explores how storytelling changes with each iteration, each explosion, each mutation. Told through multiple versions, these are stories of weapons testing, sheep that can herd themselves into watercolors, and a pregnant woman whose water breaks every day for nine months — stories told with an unexpected syntax and a sense of déjà vu: narrative as echo. "I love Dana Green's wild mind and the beautiful flux of these stories. Here the wicked simmers with the sweet, and reading is akin to watching birds. How lucky, and how glad I am, to have this book in my hands" (**NOY HOLLAND**). "Dana Green's *Sometimes the Air in the Room Goes Missing* is a tour de force of deeply destabilizing investigation into language and self, languages and selves — for the multiplicities abound here. Excitingly reminiscent at times of the work of Diane Williams and Robert Walser and Russel Edson, Green's brilliant writing is also all her own. This book is the start of something special" (**LAIRD HUNT**). "Language becomes a beautiful problem amid the atomic explosions and nuclear families and strange symmetries and southwestern deserts and frail human bodies blasted by cancer that comprise Dana Green's bracing debut, which reminds us every ordinary moment, every ordinary sentence, is an impending emergency" (**LANCE OLSEN**).

Debut author Elizabeth Hall began writing *I Have Devoted My Life to the Clitoris* after reading Thomas Laqueur's *Making Sex*. She was struck by Laqueur's bold assertion: "More words have been shed, I suspect, about the clitoris, than about any other organ, or at least, any organ its size." If Lacquer's claim was correct, where was this trove of prose devoted to the clit? And more: what did size have to do with it? Hall set out to find all that had been written about the clit past and present. As she soon discovered, the history of the clitoris is no ordinary tale; rather, its history is marked by the act of forgetting. "Marvelously researched and sculpted.... Bulleted points rat-tat-tatting the patriarchy, strobing with pleasure" (DODIE BELLAMY). "Freud, terra cotta cunts, hyenas, anatomists, and Acker, mixed with a certain slant of light on a windowsill and a leg thrown open invite us... Bawdy and beautiful" (WENDY C. ORTIZ). "Gorgeous little book about a gorgeous little organ... Mines discourses as varied as sexology, plastic surgery, literature and feminism to produce an eye-opening compendium.... The 'tender button' finally gets its due" (JANET SARBANES). "God this book is glorious.... You will learn and laugh and wonder why it took you so long to find this book" (SUZANNE SCANLON).

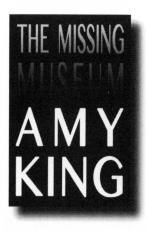

Nothing that is complicated may ever be simplified, but rather cata-
logued, cherished, exposed. *The Missing Museum*, by acclaimed poet
Amy King, spans art, physics & the spiritual, including poems that
converse with the sublime and ethereal. They act through ekphrasis,
apostrophe & alchemical conjuring. They amass, pile, and occasionally
flatten as matter is beaten into text. Here is a kind of directory of the
world as it rushes into extinction, in order to preserve and transform
it at once. King joins the ranks of Ann Patchett, Eleanor Roosevelt
& Rachel Carson as the recipient of the 2015 Women's National
Book Association Award. She serves on the executive board of VIDA:
Women in Literary Arts and is currently co-editing the anthologies
*Big Energy Poets of the Anthropocene: When Ecopoets Think Climate
Change*, and *Bettering American Poetry 2015*. Of King's previous collection, *I Want to Make You Safe* (Litmus Press), John Ashbery de-
scribes Amy King's poems as bringing "abstractions to brilliant, jagged
life, emerging into rather than out of the busyness of living." *Safe* was
one of *Boston Globe*'s Best Poetry Books of 2011.

THE GROTESQUE CHILD
a novel by
KIM PARKO

The Grotesque Child is a story about being and being and being something else. It is about swallowing and regurgitating, conceiving and birthing. It is about orifices and orbs. It is about the viscous, weepy, goopy, mucousy, bloody state of feminine being and trans-being. It is about pain and various healers and torturers, soothers and inflictors. It is about what sleeps and hides in all the nooks and crannies of perceived existence and existence unperceived. Kim Parko is the author of *Cure All*, published by Caketrain Press. She lives with her husband, daughter, and the seen and unseen, in Santa Fe, New Mexico where she is an associate professor at the Institute of American Indian Arts. Praise for *Cure All*: "Parko's work flickers with pieces of word wizardry while igniting a desire to absorb the strange and distorted.... Giving insight into the human mind and heart is what Parko does best" (*DIAGRAM*)

A MEMOIR
AARON APPS

A Small Press Distribution Bestseller and Staff Pick, chosen by Dennis Cooper for his "Favorite Nonfiction of 2015," and chosen by *Fabulously Feminist Magazine* for its "Nonfiction Books You Need to Read," Aaron Apps's *Intersex* explores gender as it forms in concrete and unavoidable patterns in the material world. What happens when a child is born with ambiguous genitalia? What happens when a body is normalized? *Intersex* provides tangled and shifting answers to both of these questions as it questions our ideas of what is natural and normal about gender and personhood. In this hybrid-genre memoir, intersexed author Aaron Apps adopts and upends historical descriptors of hermaphroditic bodies such as "freak of nature," "hybrid," "imposter," "sexual pervert," and "unfortunate monstrosity" in order to trace his own monstrous sex as it perversely intertwines with gender expectations and medical discourse. "*Intersex* is all feral prominence: a physical archive of the 'strange knot.' Thus: necessarily vulnerable, brave and excessive....I felt this book in the middle of my own body. Like the best kind of memoir, Apps brings a reader close to an experience of life that is both 'unattainable' and attentive to 'what will emerge from things.' In doing so, he has written a book that bursts from its very frame" (BHANU KAPIL).

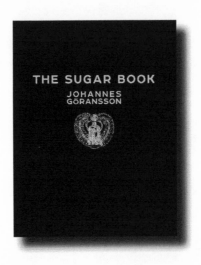

THE SUGAR BOOK
JOHANNES GÖRANSSON

Johannes Goransson's *The Sugar Book* marks the author's third title with TS Press, following his acclaimed *Haute Surveillance* and *entrance to a colonial pageant in which we all begin to intricate.* "Doubling down on his trademark misanthropic imagery amid a pageantry of the unpleasant, Johannes Göransson strolls through a violent Los Angeles in this hybrid of prose and verse.... The motifs are plentiful and varied ... pubic hair, Orpheus, law, pigs, disease, Francesca Woodman ... and the speaker's hunger for cocaine and copulation..... Fans of Göransson's distorted poetics will find this a productive addition to his body of work" (*PUBLISHERS WEEKLY*); "Sends its message like a mail train. Visceral Surrealism. His end game is an exit wound" (*FANZINE*); "As savagely anti-idealist as Burroughs or Guyotat or Ballard. Like those writers, he has no interest in assuring the reader that she or he lives, along with the poet, on the right side of history" (*ENTROPY MAGAZINE*); "convulses wildly like an animal that has eaten the poem's interior and exterior all together with silver" (**KIM HYESOON**); "'I make a language out of the bleed-through.' Göransson sure as fuck does. These poems made me cry. So sad and anxious and genius and glarey bright" (**REBECCA LOUDON**).

CLAIRE DONATO
BURIAL

The debut novella from Claire Donato that rocked the small press world. "Poetic, trance-inducing language turns a reckoning with the confusion of mortality into readerly joy at the sensuality of living." (*PUBLISHERS WEEKLY* "BEST SUMMER READS"). "A dark, multivalent, genre-bending book.... Unrelenting, grotesque beauty an exhaustive recursive obsession about the unburiability of the dead, and the incomprehensibility of death" (*PUBLISHERS WEEKLY* STARRED REVIEW). "Dense, potent language captures that sense of the unreal that, for a time, pulls people in mourning to feel closer to the dead than the living.... [S]tartlingly original and effective" (*MINNEAPOLIS STAR-TRIBUNE*). "A grief-dream, an attempt to un-sew pain from experience and to reveal it in language" (*HTML GIANT*). "A full and vibrant illustration of the restless turns of a mind undergoing trauma.... Donato makes and unmakes the world with words, and what is left shimmers with pain and delight" (BRIAN EVENSON). "A gorgeous fugue, an unforgettable progression, a telling I cannot shake" (HEATHER CHRISTLE). "Claire Donato's assured and poetic debut augurs a promising career" (BENJAMIN MOSER).

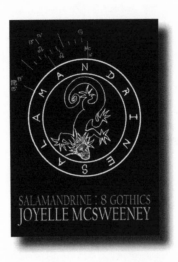

SALAMANDRINE : 8 GOTHICS
JOYELLE MCSWEENEY

Following her debut novel from Tarpauin Sky Press, the acclaimed
SPD bestseller *Nylund, The Sarcographer*, comes Joyelle McSweeney's
first collection of short stories, *Salamandrine: 8 Gothics*. "Vertiginous....
Denying the reader any orienting poles for the projected reality....
McSweeney's breakneck prose harnesses the throbbing pulse of
language itself" (**PUBLISHERS WEEKLY**). "Biological, morbid, fanatic,
surreal, McSweeney's impulses are to go to the rhetoric of the maternity
mythos by evoking the spooky, sinuous syntaxes of the gothic and the
cleverly constructed political allegory. [A]t its core is the proposition
that writing the mother-body is a viscid cage match with language and
politics in a declining age.... [T]his collection is the sexy teleological
apocrypha of motherhood literature, a siren song for those mothers
'with no soul to photograph'" (**THE BROOKLYN RAIL**). "[L]anguage
commits incest with itself.... Sounds repeat, replicate, and mutate in her
sentences, monstrous sentences of aural inbreeding and consangeous
consonants, strung out and spinning like the dirtiest double-helix, dizzy
with disease...." (**QUARTERLY WEST**).

HOSPITALOGY
DAVID WOLACH

david wolach's fourth book of poetry, *Hospitalogy*, traces living forms of intimate and militant listening within the Hospital Industrial Complex—hospitals, medical clinics and neighboring motels—performing a sociopoetic surgery that is exploratory, not curative. "An extraordinary work.... [A] radical somatics, procedural anatomic work, queer narrativity—where 'the written is explored as catastrophe and its aftermath'" **(ERICA KAUFMAN)**. "Dear 'distractionary quickie,' Dear 'groundwater,' Dear 'jesus of the pain.' Welcome to david wolach's beautiful corrosion, *Hospitalogy*" **(FRED MOTEN)**. "At a time when hospitality is increasingly deployed to sterilize policies of deportation and incarceration…david wolach performs the common detention of patients, workers, and other undesirables in 'places of liquidation' **(ELENI STECOPOULOS)**. "This is a book that documents the soft rebellion of staying alive, articulating the transition from invisibility to indecipherability" **(FRANK SHERLOCK)**.

In her second SPD bestseller from Tarpaulin Sky Press, *not merely because of the unknown that was stalking toward them*, Jenny Boully presents a "deliciously creepy" swan song from Wendy Darling to Peter Pan, as Boully reads between the lines of J. M. Barrie's *Peter and Wendy* and emerges with the darker underside, with sinister and subversive places. *not merely because of the unknown* explores, in dreamy and dark prose, how we love, how we pine away, and how we never stop loving and pining away. "This is undoubtedly the contemporary re-treatment that Peter Pan deserves.... Simultaneously metaphysical and visceral, these addresses from Wendy to Peter in lyric prose are scary, sexual, and intellectually disarming" (*HUFFINGTON POST*). "[T]o delve into Boully's work is to dive with faith from the plank — to jump, with hope and belief and a wish to see what the author has given us: a fresh, imaginative look at a tale as ageless as Peter himself" (*BOOKSLUT*). "Jenny Boully is a deeply weird writer—in the best way" (*ANDER MONSON*).

MORE FROM TARPAULIN SKY PRESS

FULL-LENGTH BOOKS

Jenny Boully, *[one love affair]**

Ana Božičević, *Stars of the Night Commute*

Traci O Connor, *Recipes for Endangered Species*

Mark Cunningham, *Body Language*

Danielle Dutton, *Attempts at a Life*

Sarah Goldstein, *Fables*

Johannes Göransson, *Entrance to a colonial pageant in which we all begin to intricate*

Noah Eli Gordon & Joshua Marie Wilkinson, *Figures for a Darkroom Voice*

Gordon Massman, *The Essential Numbers 1991 - 2008*

Joyelle McSweeney, *Nylund, The Sarcographer*

Joanna Ruocco, *Man's Companions*

Kim Gek Lin Short, *The Bugging Watch & Other Exhibits*

Shelly Taylor, *Black-Eyed Heifer*

Max Winter, *The Pictures*

Andrew Zornoza, *Where I Stay*

CHAPBOOKS

Sandy Florian, *32 Pedals and 47 Stops*

James Haug, *Scratch*

Claire Hero, *Dollyland*

Paula Koneazny, *Installation*

Paul McCormick, *The Exotic Moods of Les Baxter*

Teresa K. Miller, *Forever No Lo*

Jeanne Morel, *That Crossing Is Not Automatic*

Andrew Michael Roberts, *Give Up*

Brandon Shimoda, *The Inland Sea*

Chad Sweeney, *A Mirror to Shatter the Hammer*

Emily Toder, *Brushes With*

G.C. Waldrep, *One Way No Exit*

&

Tarpaulin Sky Literary Journal
in print and online

tarpaulinsky.com